THE ARABIAN NIGHTS

The
ARABIAN
NIGHTS

Retold by
NEIL PHILIP
Illustrated by
SHEILA MOXLEY

Orchard Books
New York

For Caro, Malcolm, and Isla
NP
In memory of my mother
SM

Text copyright © 1994 by Neil Philip
Illustrations copyright © 1994 by Sheila Moxley
Volume copyright © 1994 by The Albion Press Ltd.

First American edition

Orchard Books
95 Madison Avenue
New York, NY 10016

Manufactured in Italy

10 9 8 7 6 5 4 3 2 1

The text of this book is set in Weiss.
The illustrations are rendered in acrylics.

Library of Congress Cataloging-in-Publication Data

Philip, Neil.
The Arabian Nights / retold by Neil Philip ; illustrated by Sheila
Moxley. — 1st American ed.
p. cm.
Summary: Sheherazade, daughter of King Shahryar's advisor, tells
her husband a different story every night to keep the king from
killing her.
ISBN 0-531-06868-4
[1. Fairy tales. 2. Folklore, Arab.] I. Moxley, Sheila, ill.
II. Arabian nights. English. Selections. III. Title.
PZ8.P54Ar 1994
[398.22]–dc20   94-9137

CONTENTS

PRAISE BE TO ALLAH, the forgiving, the compassionate. Praise be to Allah, the creator of the universe. Praise be to Allah, who knows all hidden things.

There is nothing so strange it cannot be true, and no story so unlikely it cannot be told. No story is a lie, for a tale is a bridge that leads to the truth.

There are three kinds of people in this world. The first learn from their own experience, these are the wise. The second learn from the experience of others, these are the happy. The third learn nothing at all; these are the fools.

This is the story of all stories. The wise will understand it, the happy will take delight in it, the fools will be bamboozled by it.

So listen, and learn.

HOW SHEHERAZADE MARRIED
THE KING

ONCE IN the tide and flow of ancient time, there was a king named Shahryar, who ruled his people with kindness and justice except for one terrible custom.

King Shahryar had been deceived by his wife, and when he learned of her betrayal, he slew her. "There is no truth in women," he said.

After that he ordered his wazir, his chief adviser, to find him a maiden every day. He married her, spent the night with her, and in the morning ordered the wazir to have her head chopped off. He gave these wives no chance to be untrue to him.

This went on for three years, till at last there were no young girls left, except for the two daughters of the wazir himself, Sheherazade and Dunyazad.

Now Sheherazade was a learned girl, who had stored up in her memory all the tales of the Persians, the Arabs, and the Indians. She had read the philosophers and the poets, and knew the stories of both kings and common folk. The wazir was filled with grief that such a jewel of a girl should be wasted on the pleasure of a single night. But there was nothing he could do. Sheherazade must be married to King Shahryar.

That night, as Sheherazade and Shahryar lay in bed, Sheherazade asked the king if she might bid farewell to her sister, and called Dunyazad into the room. "Sister," said Dunyazad, "as this is your final night on earth, please tell me one last story, to while away the hours of darkness."

"With pleasure," said Sheherazade, "if the king wills it."

Now the king had no need of earthly riches, but he was always eager to enlarge his mind with a story, so he gladly gave permission.

So Sheherazade took a deep breath, and began to speak.

And the first story that Sheherazade told was the tale of

THE FISHERMAN AND THE JINNI

I HAVE HEARD, O great King, that there was once a poor fisherman, with a wife and three children to support.

Every day he went down to the shore and cast in his net four times only, trusting in Allah.

Now one day, at the first cast, he caught something huge and heavy, and was hard put to drag the net ashore. But after all his toil, there was nothing in it but a dead donkey.

Nevertheless, the fisherman cried, "Allah be praised!" and cast the net again. This time, all he caught was an old clay pot full of sand and mud.

A third time he cast, and this time the net came back full of broken pots and pieces of glass.

Calling on Allah once more, the fisherman cast his net for the fourth and final time. It snagged on something in the water, and this time, no matter how he tugged and pulled, he could not free it.

So there was nothing to do but dive in, to disentangle the net from the rocks that held it.

When he had got the net free and brought it back to shore, the fisherman saw that this time he had caught a jar made of yellow copper. It was heavy — almost too heavy to lift — but there was no telling what was in it, for it was sealed with the seal of King Solomon the Great.

"What strange fish Allah has sent to my net today," exclaimed the

13

fisherman. "But whatever is in this jar, the jar itself must be worth a pretty penny."

With that, the fisherman set to work with his knife to lift off the seal, to see what was in the jar. But when he removed the seal, and looked inside the jar, there was nothing there!

Then, slowly — so slowly the fisherman scarcely noticed — smoke began to spiral up from the jar's mouth: a little trickle at first, and then great gusts and billows. The smoke swirled in the air and then formed itself into the shape of a monstrous jinni. The spirit was a fearful sight, glaring down with burning eyes.

The fisherman cowered in fear, but the jinni flinched when it saw him, and gabbled, "There is no god but Allah!" Then, speaking to the fisherman, it said, "Spare me, and I will be your slave! But I beg you, do not betray me into the hands of King Solomon, may he live forever."

"What are you talking about? King Solomon has been dead for eighteen hundred years, and the world has grown old since his day. Tell me your story."

But the jinni merely replied, "There is no god but Allah. I bring you good news, O fisherman."

"What news?" asked the fisherman.

"News of your death, most swift and terrible," replied the jinni.

"And is that your thanks," said the

14

trembling fisherman, "for my rescuing you from the depths of the ocean and freeing you from your prison?"

"This is my thanks," replied the jinni. "For the service you have done me, I will allow you to choose the manner of your own death."

"But why?" asked the fisherman.

"Listen, and I will tell you," said the jinni.

"My name is Sakhr al-Jinni. I and others of my kind rebelled against the rule of King Solomon, and made war against him. But he was the stronger. I was overpowered and brought before him, and he commanded me to bind myself in Allah's name to his service.

"I refused. So King Solomon confined me in this jar and sealed it with his seal. Then he ordered the jar to be cast into the ocean.

"For one hundred years I waited patiently in that cramping darkness for someone to come and free me. 'I shall give eternal riches to my deliverer,' I promised. But no one came.

"For another hundred years I waited, saying, 'I shall show my deliverer where riches may be found.' But no one came.

"For four hundred long years I waited, saying, 'I shall grant my deliverer three wishes.' But no one came.

"At last I outwaited my patience, and my gratitude. In the black nothingness of my prison, my anger kindled. At last I said, 'I will give my deliverer nothing but his choice of death.'

"You, O fisherman, have set me free, and therefore I will give you what I have promised. There are many ways to die: choose freely among them, and I shall grant your wish."

"This is just my luck!" said the fisherman. "It just would have to be me who freed you. But I beg you, spare my life. If you show mercy to me, surely Allah will have mercy on you."

"My mind is made up," said the jinni. "You must die."

"What must be, must be," said the fisherman, thinking on his feet, "but first, by the Most High Name, promise me to answer one question that I have."

"I promise," said the jinni.

"What I do not understand," said the fisherman, "is how you ever fitted into that copper jar. You couldn't even get one foot inside, never mind the rest of you."

"That is easy," said the jinni.

"Well, I won't believe it until I've seen it with my own eyes," replied the fisherman.

At that, the jinni began to thin back into blue smoke and spiral down into the jar. As soon as the last wisp of smoke was in, the fisherman replaced the seal. Then he jeered at the jinni, saying, "Now it is your turn to choose what manner of death you want. Otherwise, I will throw you back into the sea for the rest of time. I did you a good turn, and you wanted to repay it with evil."

"I was only joking," said the jinni. "Let me out, and I will reward you as you deserve."

"You lie," said the fisherman.

But the jinni continued to grovel and plead, and at last the fisherman made it swear in the name of Allah to do him no harm and to give him a just reward for letting it out of the jar.

The fisherman removed the seal once more, and the jinni billowed out in a cloud of smoke. Roaring and screaming, the jinni kicked the copper jar way out to sea. The fisherman nearly fainted from fright, but the jinni merely laughed, and said, "Follow me."

They walked for many miles, the fisherman trailing behind the jinni's great strides. He began to wonder if the jinni was taking him out into the wilderness to kill him after all. But at last they came to a deserted valley, in the middle of which was a lake. The jinni said, "Cast your net."

The fisherman cast his net, and caught three fish: one red, one blue, and one green. The jinni said, "Take these fish to the sultan's palace, and he will reward you. Fish here once a day, and you will always have good luck. If ever you truly need me, call me three times, and I will come. And now I have fulfilled my promise to you. Farewell!" With that, the jinni stamped its feet, and the earth swallowed it up.

The fisherman took the fish to the palace, carrying them in a jar of water on his head.

The sultan had never seen such wondrous fish, and paid the fisherman well for them, as the jinni had promised.

The sultan sent the fish down to his cook, asking her to prepare a dish worthy of such special fish. She put them in the pan and began to cook them.

At once, the wall of the kitchen opened, and a young, slender, bewitching girl came through the gap. She pointed a stick at the fish, calling, "Fish, fish, are you faithful?"

And the fish lifted their heads from the pan, crying, "Yes! We are! We are!"

Three times she asked, and three times they answered. Then she left, as strangely as she had come.

When the wazir came down to see how the meal was coming along, he found the poor cook in a terrible state. All she could do was point at the now-blackened fish and stammer out her story.

"There is some mystery here," said the wazir. He sent for the fisherman, and asked him to bring more fish of the same kind the next day.

The fisherman returned to the lake and brought back three more fish. This time, the wazir himself stayed with the cook, to see what would occur.

Everything happened as before. The wall opened up, and the girl appeared, calling, "Fish, fish, are you faithful?" The fish in turn replied, "Yes! We are! We are!"

The wazir asked the fisherman to bring more fish the following day, and this time the sultan himself joined the wazir and the cook to witness the extraordinary spectacle.

The sultan called for the fisherman and asked him, "Where do these strange fish come from?"

The fisherman replied, "From a lonely lake, not far from here."

"Take me there," said the sultan.

So the fisherman took the sultan to the lake and showed him the fish flashing red, blue, and green in the water.

"I will not rest," said the sultan, "until I have solved the mystery of this lake."

The sultan and the fisherman set off to seek the meaning of the red, blue, and green fish. They walked and walked and walked. And on the second morning of their journey, they came to a mighty palace built of black stones.

The sultan knocked at the door of this palace — once, twice, three times — but no one came. He called out, "We are wayfaring strangers, seeking shelter here," but no one answered. "The place is deserted," he said.

So they entered the black palace. It was richly furnished, but empty and silent. At its heart, they found a courtyard, where four lions made from red gold held up a fountain, which sprayed jets of water as fine as diamonds and pearls.

And at that moment, they heard the sound of a human voice. It was a young man's voice, singing; but it was a song of sorrow, not joy. The sultan and the fisherman followed the song, and came to a door covered by a curtain. Raising the curtain, they saw a young man lying on a couch. He was handsome, but his face was pale and marked with sorrow.

"Tell me," said the sultan, "why you sing so sadly. What is your story?"

The young man twitched aside the coverlet from his legs, and said, "You will forgive me if I do not rise to greet you." For from the waist down, his body was solid marble.

"Who has done this to you?" asked the sultan.

"My treacherous wife, who has betrayed me and used her magic powers to sentence me to this living death. The faithful people of my city, who would not submit to her wickedness, have suffered even more, for she turned the city into a lake, and all the inhabitants into fishes. And what is worse, the enchantment cannot be lifted save by a single jinni, named Sakhr al-Jinni, and he was bottled up and cast into the ocean long, long ago."

At this, the fisherman spoke. "If I could help you, what would you give me?" he asked.

"I would make you rich beyond your dreams," said the young man.

"And I would marry your son to my daughter, and your daughters to my sons," said the sultan.

The fisherman called out three times, "Sakhr al-Jinni! Sakhr al-Jinni! Sakhr al-Jinni! Remember the promise you gave me!" And the jinni appeared, with a roar like a mighty wind.

The jinni stretched out its great pitchfork hands and touched the young man. "Be as you were," it said, and the young man's legs turned from marble back to flesh.

Then they went down to the lake, and the jinni called out across the water, "Fish, fish, are you faithful?"

All the fish raised their heads out of the lake, crying, "Yes! We are! We are!"

"Then be as you were," said the jinni.

The lake turned back into a bustling city, and all the fish became people once more.

And so the poor fisherman got his just reward for freeing the jinni from the copper jar of King Solomon.

"But what of the faithless wife?" asked King Shahryar. "Did she get her just deserts?"

"No doubt," said Sheherazade, "for Allah reserves a fate for all."

And to prove her point, Sheherazade began to tell King Shahryar more tales from her store of stories. She spoke of women's tricks, and men's wiles, and the twists and turns of fortune. She told him of the queen of the serpents, and the three unfortunate lovers. She told him of the king's son and the ogress, and of the porter and the three ladies of Baghdad. She told him of the ugly man and his beautiful wife, and of the woman who made her husband sift dust.

Night after night, Sheherazade told her tales, and on morning after morning, King Shahryar spared her from the headsman's blade so that he could hear on the next night how her stories turned out.

Sheherazade's tales were especially welcome to the king, because his heart was so troubled that he often lay awake for long hours of the night. "If only I could get some rest," he sighed, on one such night that seemed as if it would never end. Sheherazade replied, "Perhaps, my lord, sleep would follow laughter, as it did for Harun al-Rashid." And she told him the story of

FAIR SHARES

ONE NIGHT, the caliph Harun al-Rashid was unable to sleep. He paced up and down his apartments, complaining and groaning. "Why can't I sleep? Why?" he kept exclaiming. At last his sword bearer, Masrur, couldn't keep a straight face any longer, and began to rock with laughter.

Harun al-Rashid pounced. "What are you laughing at, you impertinent jackanapes? Do you dare to laugh at me?"

"No, no!" said Masrur. "I assure you, I was only laughing as I remembered the excellent jests I heard yesterday from a jokester called Ibn al-Karibi."

"If this Ibn al-Karibi is as funny as that, I must hear him for myself," said the caliph. "Fetch him to me."

Masrur went at once to fetch Ibn al-Karibi. He roused him from his bed, saying, "Quick! The caliph wants you to make him laugh. But mind, as I've put this opportunity your way, I must have three-quarters of any reward he gives you."

"Two-thirds," said Ibn al-Karibi.

"Done," said Masrur.

"Well," said Harun al-Rashid when they returned, "so you are the famous teller of jokes. I am in a very bad temper, and I feel it would do me good to laugh. So, amuse me."

Nothing is so difficult as to tell jokes to order, and poor Ibn al-Karibi made a terrible mess of each one. He forgot the point, and muddled up one joke with another, and never raised so much as a smile.

"You're not trying!" shouted the caliph in exasperation. "Do I have to have the jokes beaten out of you?"

This threat was the last straw, and Ibn al-Karibi dried up completely, halfway through the story of the man who was granted three wishes on the Night of Power, and the foolish use he made of them.

The caliph ordered up his guards and told them, "Give this wretch a hundred blows on the soles of his feet. Perhaps that will drive the blood back up into his brain."

But after thirty-three blows, Ibn al-Karibi cried, "Stop!"

"Have you thought of a joke?" asked the caliph.

"No," replied Ibn al-Karibi. "It's just that I didn't want to steal any of Masrur's share of my reward. After all, we did agree that he should have two-thirds of anything I got; he wanted three-quarters, but I argued him down."

So Masrur took Ibn al-Karibi's place. But it took only a few blows before he, too, cried out, "Stop!"

"What it is now?" asked the caliph.

"I admit it," said Masrur. "It was unjust of me to demand two-thirds of the reward. I should have been happy with a quarter. Therefore, I give up my claim to the rest!"

And, at last, Harun al-Rashid began to laugh. As he laughed, his bad mood fell away and, instead of a hundred blows, he gave Ibn al-Karibi a hundred gold coins, and Ibn al-Karibi gave Masrur twenty-five.

And Sheherazade continued with the story of the man who never laughed, but King Shahryar did not hear it. He had fallen asleep.

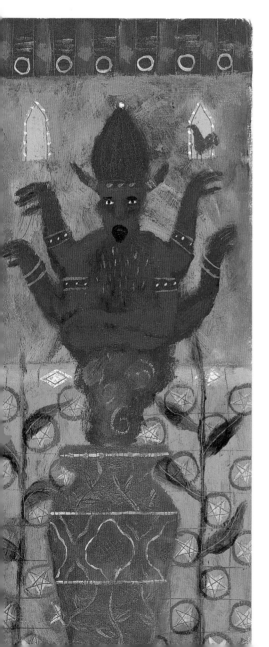

THE CITY OF BRASS

THERE WAS, in times and years long gone, a caliph of Damascus in Syria named Abd al-Malik bin Marwan, a man of a curious and scholarly turn of mind.

One day, Abd al-Malik was talking with sultans and kings and the wise men of his empire, and the talk turned to legends of King Solomon, on whom Allah bestowed mastery and dominion over men and beasts and birds, and also over the spirits of air, sea, and earth, the jinn. "I have heard," said Abd al-Malik, "that Solomon used to imprison in copper jars those jinn who defied him."

"It is true," said one of those present, Talib bin Sahl. "Even today, fishermen sometimes catch in their nets one of those very jars, sealed with the seal ring of the great King Solomon. You can hear the miserable creature within, crying, 'I repent! I repent!' If you break the seal, it writhes out of the jar in the form of smoke, before taking shape. But if you fail to extract a promise from it to obey you and to humble itself before the might of Allah the all-knowing, the freed jinni will turn on you and rend you limb from limb."

24

"I would give much to see one of these jars," said Abd al-Malik. "For surely there is a lesson in them for the wise."

So he sent Talib to Musa bin Nusayr, emir of Morocco, with a letter instructing him to seek for one of the jars.

When Musa received the letter, he said, "I hear and obey the prince of the faithful." But he had no idea where to start, and neither did Talib. So he sent for an ancient man, Sheikh Abd al-Samad, who knew many hidden things.

Sheikh Abd said, "I can take you where you will find such a jar, but it is a long and tiring journey, full of hardships and terrors."

"Then let us start without delay," said Musa bin Nusayr.

So Musa and Talib and Sheikh Abd al-Samad set out across the hot and thirsty desert, with a handful of servants and a caravan of one thousand camels laden with food and water. Day after day they journeyed, while the desert wind parched their throats and the desert sun seared their eyes.

At the end of one year, Emir Musa turned to Sheikh Abd al-Samad and, indicating the trackless wastes which surrounded them, asked, "Where are we now?"

Sheikh Abd said, "We are lost. The stars were hidden in the clouds, and we have gone astray."

"Then we must trust in Allah to guide us," said the emir.

Soon after, the men saw on the horizon a shimmer, as if there were something there, but whether it was real or an illusion they could not tell. They journeyed toward it, and soon they could see that it was a high castle, built of black stone, with a thousand steps leading up to it, and a huge dome covered with lead. All about was bare desert.

"Allah be praised," said Sheikh Abd.

They approached the castle. On its great doors was an inscription.
It read:

O you men who pass this way,
Take heed before it is too late:
We are now but dust and clay,
Who once ruled here in pomp and state.
All our former power and sway
Is ended. Allah alone is great.
You, too, will live for but a day —
For no man can outlive his fate.

"Truly, what is brought by the wind will be carried away by the wind,"
said Musa bin Nusayr.

They turned from the tomb of so many hopes and dreams, back into
the desert.

After many more days, they came to a pillar of black stone. Chained
to this was a fearful creature, half-buried in the sand. It had two great
wings, and four arms: two like a man's, and two like a lion's. In the
middle of its forehead was a third eye, which sent out sparks of fire.
The creature was moaning and lamenting.

"Tell me," said Emir Musa, "what is your name and story?"

"I am a jinni," replied the monster. "My name is Amazement, son of
Blear.

"In ancient times, this land, which now is desert, was governed by
my master, the king of the sea. It was I who inhabited the red agate
idol that guarded the City of Brass. All the folk of that land would
consult me, and I would speak from the idol, telling them, 'Do this.
Do that. Rejoice. Repent. Slay my enemies. Slay yourselves.' I
ordered them, and they obeyed.

"Of all the people, the one who adored the idol most was the
daughter of the king, the most beautiful of women. Word of her
beauty reached even to the ears of Solomon the Wise, and he sent to
the king, saying, 'Destroy this idol, admit there is no god but Allah,
and send your daughter to be my wife.'

"The king consulted me, and I laughed, in my ignorance and pride, telling him, 'Have no fear. How could this Solomon attack us here, in the middle of this great ocean, with all the armies of the jinn to fight for us?'

"So the king sent back an insolent reply to Solomon, and Solomon gathered up a great army of men and birds and beasts, and six hundred thousand devils, and attacked us. The very winds, the very waves obeyed him.

"I was condemned, as you see, to repent my ways, chained to this pillar until the day of Judgment. And all my followers of the jinn were imprisoned in copper jars, which were sealed with the seal ring of Solomon, and thrown into the sea that lapped the walls of the City of Brass."

Taking leave of the jinni, Emir Musa and his companions continued on their way, sure now that they would achieve their goal when they reached the City of Brass.

Soon they saw before them a great blackness, flanked by twin fires. Sheikh Abd said, "That is the City of Brass, and its two towers."

It was a city of dream.

Its houses and mansions and palaces and pavilions and domes slept in the moonlight. Streams rippled through scented gardens; fountains played in calm courtyards. And over all the streets and ways of the city, there was the hush of death.

Here, too, were tombs and inscriptions, and the burden of all of them was the same: vanity, vanity, all is vanity.

"Why is man born if only to die?" cried Talib.

But Emir Musa said, "Glory to Allah the most high, for he is the Forgiving One." Then Musa wept, for the littleness of man and the greatness of God, and Talib bin Sahl and Sheikh Abd al-Samad wept with him.

The companions walked slowly and sorrowfully through the streets of this city of death. Everywhere was cold marble and burning brass, high columns and cool arcades. And gradually, as they walked, the city peopled itself once again. But these were shades, not living souls: thin, silent creatures of the city's memory. Emir Musa addressed them in every language known to man, and with every gesture of greeting or

communication used in any land in which he had been, but they, being dead, had business only with the dead, and made no response.

The companions entered the great palace. They walked through marble halls on which an ever-changing light played. All around were precious jewels and weapons and treasures of earlier times.

At the end of the palace they came to a door, which led into a hall of marble so finely polished that it seemed as though the floor itself was made of flowing water. Under a canopy in the middle of this room was a couch, and on the couch a maiden slept her final sleep. Beautiful as in life she lay, with a gold crown on her head and a king's ransom of jewels about her person. Dead as she was, her eyes seemed still to hold the memory of life, and Emir Musa could not help addressing her: "Peace be with you, lady."

Guarding her rest were two soldiers, one with a mace, the other with a sword, and between them lay a golden tablet, on which was written:

In the name of Allah, the compassionate, the creator of mankind, lord of lords and causer of causes! In the name of Allah, the never-beginning, the everlasting, the ordainer of fate and fortune! Reflect, O sons of Adam, on your final end.

Where is Adam, the first of men? Where is Noah, and his sons? Where is Shaddad son of Ad? Their dwelling places are empty, and they are gone. They are dead, and turned to rotten bones.

Know that I am Tadmurah, daughter of the kings of the Amalekites, before whom all men bowed their necks. Long years I ruled here, in ease and delight. But drought came. For seven years no drop of rain fell from the skies, and the green land withered to desert. So I sent my councillors out into the world, with all the treasures that you see about you, to buy food for my people. But no food was to be had. They brought the treasures back to me, and what we once thought priceless, we now disdained as worthless trinkets.

So we all died, and here I sleep until the day of Judgment. Take what you will from our treasure hoards, if you still value worldly wealth, but do not disturb my rest.

Allah is most great!

Emir Musa told the servants who were with them to gather up the treasures in the palace and load them onto the camels. "But do not touch the princess Tadmurah, for the jewels she wears are her outfit for her last journey."

"Nonsense," said Talib. "Those jewels are no use to her. On that journey, one cotton garment will suffice." And Talib mounted the steps of the couch, and grabbed at the princess's jewels.

Emir Musa and Sheikh Abd could only watch as the two guards stirred briefly back to life. The first raised his mace and struck Talib on the back, while the second swung his sword and lopped off Talib's head.

"Allah have mercy," said Emir Musa.

With that, the emir and the sheikh left the palace, and the city, taking with them such treasure as they had gathered up.

Beyond the city, they came to the shores of the sea, and found fishermen drying nets there.

The oldest of the fishermen hailed them, saying, "Are you men, or jinn, that come from the enchanted City of Brass, where no man has lived, time out of mind?"

"We are men," said Emir Musa. "But we seek the jinn who were sealed in copper jars and thrown into this sea by King Solomon."

"We have many of these jars, which we use for cooking — once we have sworn the jinni inside to the service of Allah and released it. Stay with us for three days, and we will surely catch some more in our nets, and you are welcome to them."

Three days later, Emir Musa and Sheikh Abd started their homeward journey. Their camels were laden with jewels from the City of Brass; they had twelve copper jars, still filled with the smoke of the jinn and sealed with the seal ring of Solomon the Wise; and they carried also, as a present for the caliph Abd al-Malik bin Marwan, two mermaids, which the fishermen had also caught in their nets.

Emir Musa told the caliph all that had happened. Abd al-Malik fell silent when he heard of the death of Talib bin Sahl, but listened in wonder to the tales of their adventures.

The caliph ordered a fountain to be made for the mermaids to live

in. They knew no human tongue, but they smiled when spoken to, and sang sweetly in their own language.

Lastly, the caliph broke the seals on the twelve copper jars, conjuring the spirits within to yield to Allah. The jinn came forth in clouds of blue smoke, crying, "We repent, O Prophet of Allah! Command us! But do not send us back into the jars."

Caliph Abd al-Malik wanted no dominion over such creatures, and let them go free. As for the treasure from the City of Brass, the caliph gave some of it to Emir Musa, and some to Sheikh Abd, and divided the rest among the poor.

Sheherazade told stories night after night: all the voyages of Sinbad the Sailor, and the adventures of Land Abdullah and Sea Abdullah; the fate of the man who stole the dog's golden dish; the story of the ruined man who became rich again through a dream. And one night she told the story of

THE ANKLET

IT IS said, O King, that there were once in a city three sisters, who lived together and earned their bread by spinning flax. The youngest was also the prettiest, radiant and graceful as the moon. Her elder sisters, who were born to a different mother, hated and envied her, both for her beauty and for her skill at spinning.

One day the youngest went to market, and, finding herself with a small coin left over, bought a little clay pot to hold flowers.

"You silly girl," shrieked the sisters. "We can't waste our money on fancies and fripperies."

She made no answer, but placed a single rose in the pot, and sat down to her spinning.

The days passed, in drudgery and silent toil. The two older sisters kept nagging the poor girl and making fun of her. Her only pleasure in life was to fill the little pot with flowers, which she could look at and smell as she worked.

Now one day the sisters were out, and the girl, alone with her thoughts, burst into tears. "Oh, little pot," she said, "you are my only friend. My sisters have gone out and left me to work all by myself, without anything to eat."

And the little pot heard her, and brought forth sweetmeats for her to eat. For there was a jinni in the pot, and whatever the mistress of the pot asked for, the jinni would provide.

The girl kept the secret of the pot from her sisters, but whenever they were out, she would ask it for whatever she fancied. She would eat and drink her fill, and dress up in beautiful clothes; but when her sisters came home, she was always careful to be back in her rags and hard at work at her spinning wheel.

Now it happened that the king announced that he was going to hold a great feast for all the people of the city. Everyone was invited, even the three poor sisters.

The two older sisters dressed up in their threadbare best, and set out for the feast. "You can't come," they said. "You would shame us in those rags. You're not fit for such fine company."

But as soon as they were gone, the girl asked her pot for a beautiful green robe and scarves and garments of the finest silk. She asked, too, for sparkling rings and turquoise bracelets, and gold anklets studded with diamonds to wear around her slender ankles.

When she entered the king's harem, where the women's part of the entertainments was being held, everyone there gasped at her beauty, and at the richness of her magic clothes and jewels. Even her sisters were moved to tears at her grace and charm, and never guessed that this lovely princess was their own despised sister.

The girl slipped away before the end of the feast, so as to be home first. She took off the diamond anklets in order to be able to run faster, and in her haste she did not notice that she dropped one. It fell into the water trough where the king's horses drank.

Next morning the horses refused to drink, shying away from the trough in terror, for the anklet shone and flared beneath the water, frightening them.

The groom took the jewel to the king's son. He turned it around and around in his hands, saying nothing. Finally he declared, "The girl whom this anklet fits shall be my wife!"

He took the anklet to his mother. "Mother," he said, "you know about such things. Please find the girl to whom this anklet belongs. I am in love with her already, and long to see the anklet gracing her slim, shapely ankle."

So the queen organized a search of the whole city. She visited all the harems, and all the houses, but no one had an ankle slim enough to wear the anklet. Finally she went into the very poorest quarter, to the

house of the three sisters. The two older sisters tried in vain to force the anklet on, but when the queen tried it on the youngest, it fitted perfectly. The search was over.

The queen led the girl back to the palace. The celebrations went on for forty days and forty nights, while the wedding was prepared. At last, the day arrived, and the bride was taken to the baths by her sisters, who were to dress her.

The older girls had worried away at the poor, trusting girl until they had wheedled the secret of the magic pot from her and they, too, had made requests of the jinni. They dressed her hair with the diamond pins the jinni provided, and as the last pin went into place, the girl was turned into a white dove, which flew out the window in panic. She had been transformed by the magic pins.

When the queen asked where the bride was, the sisters just said, "She has gone."

The prince sent out search parties to scour the city for his bride, but she was nowhere to be found. Without her, he began to sicken and waste away.

Every day, at dawn and at dusk, the white dove came to the prince's window, and cooed to him in his misery. The prince grew to love the bird, which seemed to be the only creature that could soothe his lonely heart. One day he reached out to touch her and, seeing she did not fly away, took her in his hand.

The dove cooed at the prince, and he began to smooth her feathers. Noticing something hard beneath them, he scratched the place, and out fell a diamond pin. He pulled out another, and another. And when the last pin was gone, the dove ruffled her feathers and shook herself back into her true shape, his bride once more.

The prince and his love lived many years in happiness, blessed by children as beautiful and kind as themselves. But the two sisters died of jealousy, poisoned by their own spite.

THE WONDERFUL BAG

MY LORD Shahryar, you are not the only king to have whiled away his nights with stories. For it is told that the great caliph Harun al-Rashid himself, when wakeful and heavy of heart, used to send for his storyteller Ali, and beg of him some tale.

On one such night, the caliph sent for Ali, and the wily storyteller asked him, "O Commander of the Faithful, do you wish for a tale of things I have seen with my own eyes, or a tale of things I have only heard?"

"Tell me a tale of your own adventures," said the caliph.

So Ali began.

Some years ago I set out from this city of Baghdad on a journey, carrying with me only a leather bag.

As I passed through the marketplace, I paused at a stall to examine a carpet hanging there, and a rascally Kurd picked up my bag and carried it off. I ran after him and, seizing him by the arm, demanded my bag back.

"What do you mean?" he asked, bold as brass. "This is my bag, and everything in it is mine, too."

I raised an outcry then, and soon all those in the market — the hawkers, the merchants, the water carriers, the porters, even, O prince of believers, the storytellers — were gathered around us. We marched to the judge, and demanded justice.

"Which of you is the complainant?" asked the judge. And the Kurd had the impudence to step forward, elbowing me aside.

"Allah preserve your worship," he gushed. "This is my bag, and this

is my swag. I lost it yesterday, and didn't get a wink of sleep last night for worrying about it, but found it today in the keeping of this man here" — pointing at me — "who was clearly going to sneak out of the city with it."

"If the bag is yours," said the judge, "then you will be able to tell me what is in it."

"Assuredly," said the Kurd. "There is in this bag — or at least was when I lost it — a quantity of kohl eye makeup, and two silver sticks to apply it with. Also a handkerchief, and two golden cups and two candlesticks. And two plates, two spoons, and a cushion, and two leather rugs and two jugs and a brass tray and two basins and a cooking pot and two water jars and a ladle and a sacking needle and a she-cat, and a wooden trencher and two sacks and two saddles and a gown and two fur wraps and a cow and two calves and a she-goat, two sheep and two lambs, a he-camel and two she-camels, a lioness and two lions, two tents, a palace with two grand halls, a kitchen with two doors, and a whole company of Kurds ready to swear that this bag is my bag."

"And what do you have to say for yourself?" the judge asked me.

I must admit I was flabbergasted at the Kurd's speech. I told the judge, "Truly, your worship, there was nothing in this bag save a ruined house, and another without a door, and a dog kennel and a boys' school and a group of youths playing dice in a tent, and the city of Basra, and the fabled palace of Shaddad bin Ad, and a forge and a fishing net, ten untouched girls, and a thousand fancy men ready to swear that this bag is my bag."

At this the Kurd burst out weeping, and cried, "O lord, this is my bag. Besides what I told you before, this bag contains two castles and ten towers, a brood mare and two colts, a city and two villages, a blind man, a lame man and two cripples, a house of ill repute, a sea captain with his ship and crew, a Christian priest and two deacons, a patriarch and two monks, and a judge and two witnesses ready to swear that this bag is my bag."

I was nearly stumped at this, but I still had my wits about me. "Hear me, your worship," I shouted. "This bag is mine. For I keep in it my coat of chain mail, and my sword and weapons, and a thousand fighting rams, and a sheepfold and meadow, and a thousand barking dogs, and vineyards, and flower gardens filled with dancers, singers and jugglers, newlyweds and wastrels, honest men and rogues, six good jokes and a dozen foul smells, a racecourse, a mosque, a steam bath, the earthly paradise, and the kingdom of Solomon. And, I may add, a razor sharp enough to shave the beard off a judge stupid enough not to recognize that this bag is my bag."

"Each man is master of his own beard," said the judge, "and I see by what you say that you two are making fun of me, and of the law. Either that, or this wonderful bag is a bottomless pit. Let the bag be opened, and we will see what is inside it."

The bag was opened, and all that was in it was some bread and a handful of olives.

"That's not my bag," I said. "Mine must have gone astray, with all my treasures in it. This one must be the Kurd's." And with that, I went on my way.

And on another night, Sheherazade entertained Shahryar with the rogueries of
Delilah the Wily and her daughter Zaynab the Cheat, with Ahmad the Moth,
Hasan the Pest, Quicksilver Ali, and Zuraik the fried fish merchant. And when that
tale was told, she continued with the story of

JUDAR AND HIS BROTHERS

THERE WAS once a merchant named Omar who had three
sons: Sálim and Salím, who were twins, and Judar, the
youngest. He brought them all up until they reached man-
hood; and of the three, he preferred Judar. But because he loved Judar
so well, the two elder boys hated and envied their younger brother.

When Omar grew old, and knew that he would soon die, he began
to worry about what would happen to Judar after his death. So he
called all his family together and, in front of a judge, divided all his
wealth into four equal parts: one for each of the brothers, and one for
his wife, to give her a comfortable widowhood. And the next day, the
old man died.

No sooner was Omar gone than Sálim and Salím claimed part of
Judar's money for themselves. "Our father was wandering in his wits at
the end," they said. "He wouldn't have wanted his fortune to come to
you, depriving us of our rightful inheritance. After all, we are the eldest."

Judar went to the judge who had witnessed the division of Omar's
fortune, and the judge ruled that the twins had no right to any of
Judar's money. But Sálim and Salím were not satisfied, and they
dragged Judar before a second judge, and a third, and fourth, and a
fifth, until all three brothers were reduced to poverty — the costs of
these legal squabbles, especially the fat bribes to all the judges, soon
ran through their money.

Sálim and Salím, the good-for-nothing ungrateful wretches, then battened upon their poor mother. They robbed her of all her money, and drove her from her home with blows and jeers.

The poor woman came weeping to Judar's door. He told her, "Mother, do not curse my brothers. Allah, who sees and knows all, will give them their reward. Their greed has already wasted everything our father worked for and brought our family to shame. Let them keep what they have taken, and you and I will live together. If we only have a crust to eat, at least we will share that crust between us; we won't argue about it."

Judar spent his last coins on a fishing net, and every day he went to the waters of the great river Nile and cast in his net. Some days he earned ten copper pieces from his fishing, sometimes twenty, sometimes even thirty, and so he and his mother managed to live in comfort and keep themselves fed.

Sálim and Salím, however, soon ran through their mother's money and, being too lazy to work, came to Judar's door while he was out fishing. Kneeling in the dust, they begged their mother for food. They would whine and snivel and complain of their hunger, until her mother's heart melted, and she would feed them some stale bread, or the leftovers of yesterday's meal. "Eat up quick," she would say. "You mustn't be here when Judar gets back."

But one day Judar came back early and found his brothers still sitting in the house, with bread and meat before them. However, instead of cursing them and throwing them into the street, he opened his arms to them. "Welcome, my brothers," he said. "This is a blessed day! We have missed you. You should not have stayed away so long."

"We swear by Allah," replied the brothers, "it was only shame at our own misdeeds that kept us from your door."

So all was forgiven between them, and Sálim and Salím moved in with Judar and their mother.

Every day, Judar went out as usual to fish in the river Nile, while his brothers lounged about, joking and eating. But as Judar's net was always full of fish, there was enough food for all.

There came a day, however, when Judar cast his net into the water and brought it out empty. All day he fished, but never caught so much as a sprat. At last Judar turned homeward, full of sorrow.

He passed by the baker's, where he usually bought bread for the family, and the baker hailed him. "Welcome, Judar," he said. "Do you want some bread?"

Judar just stood and sighed, holding his empty net.

"Do not worry if you cannot pay," said the baker. "Take ten coppers' worth of bread, and also ten coppers to buy meat and vegetables, and pay me back tomorrow."

"On my head and eyes be it," said Judar.

The next morning Judar arose at dawn, and went straight down to the river without eating any breakfast. "Surely Allah will bless me, and enable me to pay my debt." But once again, there seemed to be no fish in the river at all.

For seven days this continued, and each day the baker, seeing Judar's empty net, gave him bread and money, telling him, "Pay me back when you can."

At last Judar, disheartened, decided to forsake the river and try his luck at Lake Karun. "Perhaps my fate will meet me there," he said.

He was just about to cast his net into the lake when he saw a Moor approaching on a mule, which was decked out in the richest finery. The Moor alighted, saying, "Peace be upon you, Judar son of Omar."

"And on you," replied Judar.

"Judar," said the Moor, "I need your help. If you give it, you shall never regret it."

"What must I do?" asked Judar.

"Swear by Allah the all-knowing to do as I ask," said the Moor, and Judar did so.

"Now," said the Moor, "tie my arms behind my back with this cord, and throw me into the lake. Then wait and see what happens. If I raise my hands out of the water before my body, cast your net and pull me out. But if I come up feetfirst, there is no hope for me. I will be dead, and will have no more use for this mule, and its harness and saddlebags. Take them to the market, and Shamayah the merchant will give you a hundred dinars for them. You can keep the money, if you also promise to keep this matter secret."

So Judar tied the Moor's arms as he requested, while the Moor called, "Tighter! Tighter!" Then he said, "Cast me into the lake," and Judar pushed him in.

Judar waited by the bank, and at last the Moor surfaced: feetfirst. So Judar, knowing that the Moor was dead, drove the mule to the bazaar and sold him to Shamayah the merchant. Shamayah, seeing the mule, cried out, "The man is dead! And only his own greed to blame." He gave Judar a hundred dinars, and told him not to talk about what had happened.

Judar walked home past the baker's, where he stopped and gave the baker a whole gold piece, saying, "Here is what I owe you."

"Peace on you," said the baker. "There is enough here to pay for bread for two days to come."

Judar called at the butcher and the vegetable stall also, and paid over a dinar to each for food, which he carried home.

His mother and brothers were waiting by the door, with hunger in their eyes. They fell on the food like scavenging animals.

Judar gave his mother the rest of the money, saying, "If you need to buy more food, use this."

That night, Judar slept well, and the following day he returned to the lake, to see what might happen.

Once again, just as Judar was about to cast his net into the water, a Moor rode up on a mule. This one was even more splendidly decked out than the first.

The Moor hailed him: "Peace be with you, O Judar son of Omar!"

"And with you," Judar replied.

The Moor asked, "Did you see a Moor here yesterday, riding a mule like this one?"

At this Judar grew frightened, thinking that he might get into trouble for drowning the first Moor, so he said, "No, I saw nothing."

"You should know," said the Moor, "that that man was my brother. Poor Judar, there is no use denying it. You tied my brother's arms behind his back, threw him into the lake, and then sold his mule to the merchant Shamayah."

"And what if I did?" stammered Judar.

"I want you to do the same to me," replied the Moor. "And if it turns

46

out for me as it did for my brother, you may take my mule to the merchant, and he will give you another hundred dinars."

So Judar tied him up, and cast him into the lake. Shortly, the Moor surfaced: feetfirst. So Judar, knowing the man was dead, took his mule to the bazaar and sold it to the merchant Shamayah for a hundred dinars. When he saw the mule, the merchant said, "So the other is dead. And nothing but his greed to blame."

Judar walked home in high spirits. "May Allah send me such a Moor every day," he prayed.

Judar gave the second hundred dinars to his mother, too. "Oh, Judar, my son," she said. "Where is all this money coming from?" And he told her about the two Moors and the merchant Shamayah. "Do not go again to Lake Karun," she said. "I fear no good can come from this."

"What?" replied Judar. "Give up this fine new trade of drowning Moors, which pays so much better than fishing ever did? I would be a fool. After all, it is by their own wish that I throw them into the lake. If I have my way, I will go on drowning them till there are no Moors left."

So on the next day, Judar went again to the lake, and once again a Moor rode up on a richly harnessed mule, and hailed him, calling, "Peace be with you, Judar son of Omar!"

I wonder how they all know my name, thought Judar, but he replied as before, "And peace on you."

"Have any other Moors passed this way?" asked the man.

"Two," replied Judar. "At their request, I tied their hands behind their backs, threw them into the lake, and, when they were drowned, sold their mules to the merchant Shamayah. I will happily perform the same service for you."

"Peace, Judar," said the Moor. "Allah appoints an end to every life." He took out a silken cord. "Now, bind my arms, and push me into the lake."

Judar waited on the shore, and at last the Moor surfaced: hands first!

"Quick, Judar," he called from the water. "Cast your net and pull me in!" And when he emerged from the water, he was holding in each hand a fish as red as coral. These he stowed in two glass jars that were in his saddlebags.

Then the Moor embraced Judar. "The blessings of Allah be upon you, brother," he cried, "for without your help, I would have drowned, and never brought these fish to shore."

"If I have truly been of service," said Judar, "I would like to ask for payment."

"Name it, and it shall be yours," said the Moor.

"The payment I should like," said Judar, "is the true story of the two drowned men, the merchant Shamayah, and these two wonderful fish as red as coral."

"The two men you drowned," said the Moor, "were my brothers: Abd al-Salam and Abd al-Ahad. My name is Abd al-Samad. The merchant Shamayah is also my brother, and his true name is Abd al-Rahim.

"Our father, Abd al-Wadud, was a great magician, who knew how to summon up imps and demons to serve him and help him solve mysteries and find hidden treasures, and he taught us many things.

"When our father died, we divided up his wealth, and his manuscripts and magical talismans, between us, until there was only one item left. This was a book, known as *The Secrets of the Ancients*, in which my father had written down the whereabouts of every treasure hidden anywhere on earth, and the solution to every mystery. There is no other book like it, and its value is beyond gold and jewels.

"Now our father had never let us see this book, and each of us wanted to possess it. For each of us had a part of his knowledge, but the book contained it all. So we began to quarrel.

"We took our dispute to a wise old man, who told us that he would award the book to the one of us who could enter the treasure-house of al-Shamardal and bring from it the celestial globe, the phial of kohl, the sword, and the seal ring. For the ring is served by a jinni called Thundering Thunderer, and whoever possesses it need fear neither king nor sultan; he may make himself master of the whole earth, if he wishes. And with the sword, one man wielding it may vanquish an entire army, for at his command the sword will spew forth lightning and fire to slay his enemies. As for the celestial globe, you may turn it in your hands and view any place on earth as if you were actually there. And if what you see displeases you, you need only turn it toward the sun and speak a word of command, and the place will be engulfed in flames. Lastly, whoever paints his eyelids with the phial of kohl can see all the hidden treasures of the earth. Therefore the old man told us that he who secures this treasure is the rightful owner of *The Secrets of the Ancients*, and that those who fail must give up all claim to it.

"We all accepted this judgment, though none of us had ever before heard of the treasure of al-Shamardal. The wise old man told us that our father himself had tried to steal the treasure, which is in the possession of the Red King, but had been thwarted by the Red King's two sons, whose help is necessary. They had fled from him, and hid themselves in Lake Karun in the form of two fish as red as coral.

"And what's more, the fish could only be caught with the help of a poor fisherman of Cairo, one Judar son of Omar, in the way that you have seen. My brothers Abd al-Salam and Abd al-Ahad both said they would try their luck, come what might, and so did I. Our brother Abd al-Rahim had no wish to be bound and thrown into the lake, so him we disguised as the merchant Shamayah so that he could purchase our mules if we should drown.

"Abd al-Salam and Abd al-Ahad, peace be upon them, were slain by the Red King's sons. But with your help I have taken them from the lake and put them into these glass jars, for they are powerful spirits, and will help us secure the treasure of al-Shamardal.

"And that, O Judar, is the tale of the two drowned brothers, the merchant Shamayah, and the two wonderful fish as red as coral.

"Now that you have heard it, come with me. We will go to the city of Fez, and there we will enter the treasure-house of al-Shamardal and help ourselves to the globe, the phial, the sword, and the seal ring. Then we shall live as lords and brothers."

The Moor gave Judar a thousand dinars to keep his mother and brothers in food and drink while he was away. After Judar had bid his mother farewell and they had commended each other to Allah's keeping, Judar mounted the mule in front of the Moor, and they set off for Morocco.

After several hours, Judar began to feel hungry, but the Moor showed no sign of stopping. At last Judar could bear it no more, and cried, "Are we never going to eat?"

At that, the Moor drew the mule to a halt, alighted, and told Judar to fetch the saddlebags.

"What do you fancy?" asked the Moor.

"Whatever there is will do me," answered Judar.

"No, no! Tell me what you'd like best."

"Bread and cheese will be fine," said Judar.

"Bread and cheese! We can fare better than that. Do you like roast chicken?"

"Yes."

"Honeyed rice?"

"Yes."

"Apricots?"

"Yes."

The Moor went through a list of every delicacy under the sun, and each time Judar answered yes. And every time Judar said yes, the Moor reached into the saddlebags and brought out the chicken, the rice, the apricots, and all the other mouthwatering dishes he mentioned. For there was a jinni in the bag, whose sole job was to prepare and serve whatever dish his master might require.

The mule on which the Moor and Judar rode was an enchanted steed, which could cover a whole year's journey in a single day; but because Judar was unused to such fast travel, the Moor held the mule back, and they only covered a month's journey each day.

On the morning of the fifth day, they came to the city of Fez. The streets were thronging with people; the Moorish lord stretched out his hand for them to kiss.

The Moor and Judar rode in state through the streets, till they came to a certain doorway. There the Moor and Judar dismounted, and the Moor struck the ground, crying, "Mule, go back where you came from."

The ground opened and swallowed the animal, and Judar gasped. "Allah preserve us," he said.

The Moor knocked, and the door was opened by a most beautiful young maiden. Her face was as bright and graceful as the new moon, and she trembled like a thirsting gazelle. The Moor greeted her, saying, "Rahmah, my daughter, let us into my chamber."

Rahmah led the way into the upper chamber, and as Judar followed her swaying hips, he told himself, "This must surely be the daughter of a king."

The chamber was richly hung and furnished, with every kind of luxury. There the Moor and Judar indulged themselves like sultans. Judar had new clothes every day, and had nothing to do but eat and drink the food provided by the jinni in the saddlebags.

But on the twenty-first day, the Moor rose from his couch, and said to Judar, "Get up. Today is the appointed day, when you must open the treasure-house of al-Shamardal."

They rode out of the city until they came to a stream. They dismounted, and the Moor had his servants erect a tent. They feasted by the running waters, and when they were done, the Moor fetched the glass jars from the saddlebags, and began to mutter over them, making strange passes with his hands.

The two fish red as coral began to plead for mercy, but the Moor continued casting his spells until the glass jars burst. The two sons of the Red King appeared, in human form, and threw themselves at the Moor's feet. "Mercy, O master of magic," they cried. "What do you want of us?"

"I want you to open up the treasure-house of al-Shamardal."

"That we cannot do without the help of a poor fisherman of Cairo, one Judar son of Omar, for so it is written."

"He stands before you," said the Moor.

"Then," said the Red King's sons, "we will do as you ask."

The Moor began to set up all his magical apparatus and sprinkle incense onto burning charcoal, to assist in the new spells he must make. He told Judar, "Once I have begun to cast this spell, I must not speak. Therefore, listen carefully, and I will tell you how to play your part in this affair.

"When I have recited the spell, the water will dry up from this riverbed and reveal a golden door. You must knock on this once, then twice, then three times, and a voice will call, 'Who knocks at the door of the treasure-house, yet does not know how to riddle its mysteries?' You must answer, 'I am Judar the fisherman, son of Omar.'

"The door will open. A man will be waiting within, sword in hand. He will command you to stretch out your neck so that he may cut off your head. This you must do; but fear not. As he raises the sword, he will fall down dead at your feet, and you will come to no harm. But if you refuse him, he will kill you.

"Then you will find a second door. Knock again. A voice will call, 'Who knocks at the door?' and you must answer as before. This time, a horseman will be behind the door, aiming his lance at your breast. He will charge at you. If you flinch, he will surely kill you. Stand your ground, and he, too, will fall dead at your feet.

"Then you will come to a third door. This will be opened by a man with a bow and arrows. If you resist him, he will kill you. Let him take aim and fire, and he will fall dead like the others.

"Then you will come to a fourth door. Behind it, a raging lion will leap at you. Put your hand into its open jaws, and it will fall down dead. Flee it, and it will maul you.

"The fifth door will be opened by a servant. Tell him your name, and he will say, 'If you are that man, open the sixth door.'

"At the sixth door, you must cry, 'Jesus, tell Moses to open the door.' The door will fly open to reveal two dragons, who will attack you. Reach out to them, and when their mouths close around your hands, they will fall dead.

"Then go to the seventh door, and knock. It will be opened by your mother, who will greet you and try to embrace you. But you must tell her to keep her distance and order her to strip off her clothes. She will wheedle and plead, and call on you as her son to spare her, but you must insist. Only when she casts aside her final garment will the enchantment be dissolved. Then you may enter the treasure-house.

"There you will see great heaps of gold. Ignore them. Go straight to the little pavilion in the middle of the room, raise the curtain, and you will see the enchanter al-Shamardal, asleep upon a throne of gold. And there you will find the four talismans: the celestial globe, the phial of kohl, the sword, and the seal ring. Bring these to me. Take nothing else and touch nothing else.

"Do you understand?"

"I understand," stammered Judar, "but my knees have given way! No man could face such horrors and live."

"Fear not," said the Moor. "They are mere soulless images, and not true creatures. Put your trust in Allah, and they cannot harm you. But if you forget my instructions, or fail to follow them, it will be the worse for you."

With that, the Moor began his conjuring. The river dried up, and Judar approached the first door. All happened as the Moor had said, and Judar, although terrified, kept his nerve. At last he went through the seventh door, which was opened, as predicted, by his mother.

"Son," she said. "Welcome to this place. Come, let me embrace you."

"Keep away, nameless spirit," he cried.

"O son, do you not recognize your own mother?"

"Take off your clothes."

"Surely, son, you would not strip your own mother naked."

"Strip, or I will strike off your head."

Whimpering and pleading all the while, the spirit did as he instructed. But when only one garment was left, she looked up at Judar, and said, "Surely I have done enough. If your heart is not made of stone, leave me this one rag to cover my modesty."

Judar's resolve weakened. "You are right," he said. "Keep it on."

At once she cried, "He has faltered! Beat him! Beat him!" And the unseen guardians of the treasure rained blows upon him and chased him from the place.

When the Moor saw Judar flung out of the door, he rescued him from the river, and recited spells over him to bring him around.

"Alas, what have you done?" he asked.

"I broke all the enchantments," answered Judar, "but I failed at the last. I took pity on my mother, and as a result I have been thrashed within an inch of my life."

"You fool!" said the Moor. "You have made a bad mistake. Now we must wait a whole year for another chance at the treasure."

With that, they returned to the city, where they lived in luxury as before, until a year had passed. Then the Moor led Judar back to the river, and prepared his spells as before.

"This time, do not waver!" he said. "Let me tell you once again what you must do."

"No need!" said Judar. "I won't forget your instructions until I forget the thrashing I received for disobeying them last year."

"Go then," said the Moor, "and remember that the old woman is but a spirit."

Judar once again entered the golden door, and as before he faced the various spirits boldly, and passed them all, till he came to the seventh door, and met once again the spirit in the shape of his mother.

This time, he was pitiless. Though she whined and begged, he ordered her to strip stark naked. And when she had done so, she frayed back into air, a creature without a body or a soul.

Then Judar entered the hall of treasures. Gold lay in heaps about him, but he left it alone, and went instead to the pavilion where al-Shamardal lay slumbering on his throne of gold. As Judar took up the four talismans he had been sent for — the ring, the sword, the phial, and the globe — the whole room began to ring with music, and voices called, "Hail, Judar son of Omar!"

The Moor was delighted to see Judar appear with the treasures, and they returned together to the city of Fez to feast and rejoice. Then the Moor said, "My brother Judar, you left your home to help me win this treasure. Now that you have succeeded, ask what you will of me, and it shall be yours."

"I would like the saddlebags," said Judar.

"Take them, and welcome," said the Moor. "You have chosen wisely, for now you and yours will never be hungry. But had you asked for anything else, I would have given it. Therefore take also these bags of jewels, so that when you return home it will be as a rich man."

So Judar returned to Cairo, with the enchanted saddlebags and a store of gold and jewels. At the city gate, he saw his old mother squatting in the dust, begging alms in the name of Allah. He embraced her and took her home, asking her, "Mother, why are you begging? I left you with sufficient money for both you and my brothers."

"They cheated me," she replied. "They took the money you left and drove me to beg on the streets, or otherwise starve to death."

"Well," said Judar, "that at least is a fate that will never befall you."

"But I am faint with hunger, and there is no food in the house," said his mother.

"These saddlebags can supply all our wants," replied Judar. "Just ask for whatever you fancy."

"I think I could manage a crust of warm bread and a slice of cheese," said his mother.

"That's not fit for a homecoming feast," said Judar. "We shall have choice cuts of meat, and roast chicken, peppered rice, and stuffed cucumbers. We shall have tender lamb stuffed with apricots, and to follow we shall find a corner for some almond cakes, honey, and nuts."

"Don't make fun of your old mother," she replied. "You know there is no such food in the house."

"Hand me my saddlebags," said Judar.

Judar took the saddlebags, and declaimed, "O servant of the saddlebags, I conjure you by the virtue of the Mighty Names, bring me some stuffed ribs of lamb."

Judar and his mother ate dish after dish from the wonderful saddlebags, and at last she asked him how, when the saddlebags always seemed empty, they could contain such abundance. So Judar told her the secret of the bags, and his mother, much daring, plunged her hand inside. "O servant of the saddlebags," she croaked, in a wavery voice, "bring me another helping of ribs."

Then Judar's mother remembered, "I never had my warm crust and slice of cheese, and say what you like, you can't beat fresh bread and good cheese." So she ordered the jinni to bring her some. And after that, neither she nor Judar could eat another scrap.

They were lying back amid the wreckage of their feast when Judar's brothers, Sálim and Salím, came home. They had heard of Judar's return and, knowing his soft heart, guessed they could weasel their way back into his affections. And sure enough, despite all that they had done, Judar welcomed them, and bade them sit and eat.

The brothers were thin and half-starved, and didn't need asking twice. When they had eaten their fill, Judar told them, "Take what is left of the feast and give it to the poor."

"Surely we should keep it for our own supper," they replied.

"Do not worry about that; there will be plenty for all," he answered.

So the brothers did as they were told and, sure enough, that night Judar provided them with a feast of forty rare and delicate dishes, fit for the table of a sultan.

For ten whole days the brothers stuffed themselves. And all that time they wondered just how Judar kept them supplied with such glorious food, morning, noon, and night, when he never seemed to go to the market or to do any cooking. At last, when Judar was out, they persuaded their mother to tell them the secret of the enchanted saddlebags.

It wasn't long then before the brothers began to mutter to each other, "Why should we creep and crawl to Judar, and thank him kindly for throwing us these scraps like a rich man to a beggar? We are just as worthy as he to own the saddlebags."

And at last Sálim said to Salím, "Let us sell Judar as a slave to the chief captain of the Sea of Suez."

So they went to the captain and told him, "We two have another brother, a good-for-nothing wastrel. Having squandered his portion of our inheritance, roistering through the city without thought for the morrow, now he seeks to reduce us to beggary. There is nothing to be done with such a fellow. Therefore, we would like you to buy him from us, and take him to sea. He's strong enough, despite his evil ways, and you can get good work from him."

So the captain agreed to buy Judar for forty dinars, and that night the brothers brought him and two sailors back to the house, and when Judar was asleep, they seized him and dragged him to the ship. They took him to Suez, where they shackled him and set him to work as a

galley slave. For the course of a whole year, Judar worked thus, in silence and bitter shame.

Meanwhile, when Judar's mother discovered him missing, she began to wail and weep. The two brothers, Sálim and Salím, told her, "Don't make such a fuss. Judar couldn't even be bothered to tell you he was going off with those sailors in search of hidden treasure. He has left you once again, while we have stayed behind like dutiful sons." But she was not deceived, and continued to weep for Judar. At that the brothers grew angry, telling her, "You would not weep for us," and they shouted at her and beat her shamefully.

The brothers hunted out all the gold and jewels that the Moor had given to Judar, and cackled to each other over their newfound riches. Their mother told them that the treasure belonged to Judar, but they scorned her, saying, "Nonsense. This is our inheritance from our father."

Then the brothers found the enchanted saddlebags, and began to argue over them. Sálim grabbed one end, and Salím grabbed the other, and they tugged and tussled, shouting and screaming and making such a commotion that an officer of the king's guards, passing by, stopped to see what all the fuss was about.

The officer hauled the brothers off to the king, who soon bullied the truth out of them. He kept the treasure and the saddlebags for himself, clapped Sálim and Salím into prison, and awarded a pension to the mother.

As for Judar, at the end of a year, the ship in which he was rowing was caught in a terrible storm. Everyone on board was drowned, save Judar, who was cast up on the shore.

And there, for so Allah orders the fates of men, the bedraggled, wretched Judar met once again the Moor for whom he had risked his life in the treasure house of al-Shamardal. The Moor took pity on Judar, and said to him, "My brother, take the seal ring of al-Shamardal. It is served by a powerful jinni, Thundering Thunderer, who will do your bidding. With his help, you may restore your fortunes."

Judar rubbed the ring, and Thundering Thunderer appeared. "Command me, master," he roared. "Would you have me people a ruined city, or ruin a populous one? Slay a king? Rout a host? Command me!"

"Take me home," said Judar.

In Cairo, Judar learned from his mother all that had happened. "Do not worry, mother," he said. "All will be well." And he commanded the jinni Thundering Thunderer to fetch forth his brothers from their prison cell. Thundering Thunderer sank into the earth, emerged in the foul darkness of the prison, seized Sálim and Salím by the scruffs of their necks, and hauled them back to Judar's house.

When Judar saw his brothers, quaking with fear and cowering on the ground before him, his heart softened once more. "Rise, brothers, and welcome home," he said. "I must forgive you, for Allah, who knows all, forgives all."

Then Judar summoned Thundering Thunderer once again, and told him, "Go to the king's treasury, and bring me back my gold and my jewels and the enchanted saddlebags. And while you are there, gather up everything else that is hoarded there, and bring it to me. Leave nothing but the dust."

And when the jinni returned, Judar commanded him, "Build me tonight a grand palace, its walls overlaid with liquid gold and its rooms furnished beyond the dreams of kings." And this, too, the jinni achieved.

Judar, his mother, and his brothers moved into the palace, to live like sultans.

Meanwhile, the king had discovered that his treasury was bare. He felt his mind tremble in his head with rage. "Who has done this thing?" he bellowed.

"I do not know," replied his wazir, "but I can tell you that the brothers Sálim and Salím have escaped from prison, and furthermore that a glorious new palace has arisen overnight. Word has reached me that their brother Judar has returned to Cairo. Doubtless this is his work."

"Then he must die," pronounced the king. "Send an emir with fifty soldiers to deal with this upstart."

"Patience, O king," said the wazir. "Do not provoke him. A man who can build a palace in a single night, ransack your treasury, and release prisoners from your deepest dungeons must be approached with care. Let the emir ask him to a banquet. I will sound him out. If he is strong, we will defeat him by guile; if he proves weak, we will hang him, as you desire."

So the emir and fifty men were sent to ask Judar to come to the palace. However, the emir, a proud and foolish fellow, was not prepared to deal with Thundering Thunderer. The jinni was lounging on the steps of the gilded palace, in the guise of a servant. When the emir told him to fetch his master, the jinni just yawned and stretched himself out more comfortably. "Insolent dog," cried the emir, "do you think to trifle with me?"

The emir drew his sword, but Thundering Thunderer took it from him as easily as from a child, and beat him with the flat of the blade.

Wielding the sword with all his terrible strength, Thundering Thunderer beat the emir and his fifty soldiers all through the streets of Cairo till they came back, empty-handed, to the king's palace.

The king sent the emir back with a hundred men, then with two hundred, then with five hundred, but each time it was the same. Eventually the king turned to his wazir, and said, "Go yourself, and take the whole army with you."

But the wazir, being wise and cunning, said, "I would rather go alone."

The wazir approached Judar's palace humbly. He was greeted by Thundering Thunderer, who asked, "What do you want, O human?"

Knowing that he was dealing with a jinni, the wazir abased himself in the dust. "Is your master, Judar, within?" he asked.

"He is," said the jinni.

"I beg you, lord, to tell him that the king salutes him, and invites him to the palace for a banquet."

"If the king wishes to meet my master, let him come here," replied the jinni.

So the king dressed in all his majesty, and went to Judar's palace. Judar saw him coming, and commanded Thundering Thunderer to line the way with a double rank of fierce demons dressed as soldiers.

When the king saw these tall, proud figures, his heart quailed. Then he entered the palace and found Judar sitting like a sultan, and his knees gave way. He fell down before Judar, begging, "Forgive me, lord. It was pride, not justice, that caused me to lock up your brothers, and greed, not fairness, that made me steal your treasure and your saddlebags. Remember the saying, lord Judar: if there were no offending, there could be no forgiving."

"It is true," replied Judar. "Allah pardon you. Be seated." And Judar ordered a feast to be spread for the king, and also required Thundering Thunderer to return to the treasury everything that belonged to the king.

Though Judar and the king became friends in this way, still the king did not forget how he had had to humble himself to the son of a mere merchant. One day he took his wazir aside, saying, "I fear that Judar will kill me and take my throne."

"Fear not," said the wazir. "Judar is more rich and powerful than any king; your throne would mean nothing to such as he. But if you are worried, marry him to your daughter, and share your throne with him. Make him your equal."

"How could this be managed?" asked the king.

"Ask him to visit you," replied the wazir. "While we are feasting, arrange for your daughter, dressed in all her finery, to pass the open door of the room. Even a glimpse of her beauty would turn a young man's heart. He will ask me who she is; I will tell him; he will beg you for her hand. When he is married to her, you will be safe; and if, by chance, he should die, you would inherit all he has."

The king did as the wazir suggested, and all fell out as they planned. When Judar saw the king's daughter, Princess Asiyah, a shudder of longing ran through him. He was enthralled with one look. He begged the king for her hand, and the king agreed.

Years passed, and eventually the old king died, and Judar became king in his stead. He appointed his brothers Sálim and Salím his joint wazirs.

But even this mark of trust was not enough for Sálim and Salím. Soon they began to grumble to each other, "We do all the work, while Judar just sits on his throne, giving us orders. Why should we slave for him, when by rights the treasure and the saddlebags, and the seal ring should be ours. After all, we are older than Judar."

Salím told Sálim, "You are more cunning than I. Surely you can come up with a plan to get rid of him."

"If I do," said Sálim, "I must be king, and keep the ring; but you can be wazir, and keep the saddlebags." And Salím agreed.

So, driven by greed, they set a trap for their brother Judar. They invited him to a feast in Sálim's apartments and fed him poison, so that he sickened and died. Then Sálim, lusting for power over Thundering Thunderer, pulled at the ring on Judar's finger, but it was jammed on; so Sálim cut off the finger to get the ring.

Sálim rubbed the ring, and the jinni appeared. "Command me, O master," it said.

"Take my brother Salím and put him to death," said Sálim.

Then Sálim commanded Thundering Thunderer to show the bodies of Judar and Salím to the people, announcing, "Such will be the fate of all who stand in my way."

Sálim declared himself king, and his first decree was that he would marry Asiyah. He was told, "You must wait until the months of her widowhood are passed," but he replied, "Such fooleries mean nothing to me. I will marry her tonight."

So that night Asiyah was brought to his chamber. Her eyes were red from weeping for her beloved Judar, but she disguised them with kohl; her hands were trembling with fear and loathing, but she pretended it was passion. She smiled on her new husband, and brought him a cup of wine; but there was poison in the cup, and when Sálim drank it, he fell lifeless to the ground, a soulless husk.

Sheherazade fell silent, and turned to the king.

"There is no need to tell me what happened next," he said. "No doubt this Asiyah soon married again, and her husband ruled, through the power of the seal ring and the saddlebags."

"No," said Sheherazade. "Asiyah never remarried, for where could she have found a man the match of Judar? She spent the rest of her life in prayer and contemplation. But first she made sure that never again would the seal ring and the saddlebags tempt the ambitious and greedy to theft and murder.

"She took the ring and broke it in two, that no one else might ever possess it, and took the saddlebags and destroyed them likewise.

"And that," said Sheherazade, "is all I know of the tale of Judar the trustful and his treacherous brothers, Sálim and Salím."

The tale of Judar and his brothers displeased King Shahryar, for it reminded him of how love can be repaid with hate, and trust with treachery. "You have entertained me well," he said, "but the time has come for you to die. Tomorrow, the headsman will do his work."

"As you wish, my lord," said Sheherazade. "Allah knows all ends. I am just sorry not to have time to tell you the magical tale of the ebony horse, and the love of Kamar al-Akmar and Shams al-Nahar. But perhaps you already know it."

"That is a tale which I have never heard," said King Shahryar.

So Sheherazade began to tell the story of

THE EBONY HORSE

ONCE THERE was a great king of the Persians, Sabur by name, who was the king of all kings for wisdom, learning, and justice; lover of the poor; and friend to the broken-hearted. He had three daughters, like three full moons in the night sky, and a son, Kamar al-Akmar, who was the star of stars.

Now Sabur loved all inventions and clever devices, and the wise men of his day vied to produce things that would interest and amuse him. One feast day, he was sitting on his throne when three men, each masters of the occult sciences, approached him.

The first was an Indian, who prostrated himself before the throne. He offered Sabur his gift, which was a golden statue of a man, covered in jewels, holding in his hand a golden trumpet.

"This is fine work," said Sabur, "but does it have some hidden virtue?"

"It does, my lord," replied the Indian. "Set this figure at the gate of the city, and it will be a guardian of the peace. If an enemy should enter, it will blow on the trumpet, and the enemy will fall down dead."

Then the second man, a Greek, approached the throne. His gift was a silver basin, in which there was a gold peacock surrounded by twenty-four gold peahens. "My lord," he said, "through the day, the peacock will peck each peahen in turn, to mark out the hours. And at the end of each month, the peacock will open its mouth, and reveal the new crescent moon in its throat."

Finally the third man, a Persian, stepped forward. He presented the king with a full-size horse made out of the blackest ebony wood, inlaid with gold and jewels, saddled and harnessed after the manner of kings. "My lord," he said, "if you mount this horse, it will carry you wherever you want through the air. And, what's more, it can cover a whole year's journey in a single day."

"This is the best of all," exclaimed the king. "By Allah, if what you say is true, all three of you shall be rewarded with your hearts' desires."

The king decided to try out his new gifts at once. The golden man was installed as a sleepless watchman on the city gate. Sure enough, when an enemy tried to enter the city that night to kill the king, the golden man saw him and blew such a blast on his trumpet that the man fell down dead with fright.

The gold peacock faithfully marked all the hours of the day and, the next day beginning a new month, opened its mouth to reveal the crescent moon.

Most magical of all, the Persian sage mounted the ebony horse and rode it high into the sky. He circled the city, and then descended again.

"Now," said the king, "name your rewards."

The sages replied, "If you are pleased with our gifts, we would ask for your daughters' hands in marriage."

"Be it so," said the king.

Now the king's three daughters were watching and listening behind a curtain and, when they heard this, looked more closely at their husbands-to-be. The oldest daughter chose the Indian, and he was a well-made man. The middle daughter chose the Greek, and he was handsome enough. But the youngest daughter was left with the Persian, and he was a hundred years old if he was a day. His straggly hair was frosted white, his eyebrows were moth-eaten, and his beard was stained with dribble. His forehead drooped; his bleary eyes goggled; his nose was flabby and red; his lips hung trembling down like a camel's; his few remaining teeth were crooked and broken like the fangs of a demon. Altogether he was the ugliest, most grotesque and repulsive man she had ever seen.

The king's youngest daughter was one of the fairest and most graceful of maidens, slender as a gazelle, delicate as the breeze, and brighter than the moon. When she saw her husband-to-be, she let out a sharp cry, like one who has been dealt a deadly wound, and ran, weeping, to her chamber.

Her brother, Prince Kamar al-Akmar, hearing her tormented cries, came in to her, asking, "What is the matter?"

She told him, "Our father has promised me in marriage to a foul magician who has bewitched him with the gift of an ebony horse. I wish I were dead!"

Prince Kamar al-Akmar went to his father and asked him, "Father, is it true that you have thrown your most precious jewel onto a dung heap?"

The Persian, hearing this, trembled with rage.

The king replied, "Son, if you had seen the magic horse that this man has made, you would understand that he is truly worthy of your sister's hand. It is an amazing thing."

So the horse was brought to them, and the prince, being a skilled horseman, swung himself into the saddle.

"How do you make it go?" he asked.

"Lord," replied the Persian, "if you pull the pin on the right-hand flank, the horse will ascend; you direct it with the reins."

The prince pulled the pin, and the horse rose into the air, flying so high that it disappeared from view.

The king waited on the ground for his son to return, but, though he eagerly scanned the sky, there was no sign of him. He turned, troubled, to the Persian. "How will the prince descend?" he asked.

"O king," replied the sage, "the prince, in his pride, did not stop to ask me that question. I had no time to show him the pin of descent. Therefore I fear you will not see your son again until the day of Resurrection."

The king made no reply to this, but ordered his guards to seize the Persian and clap him into jail.

Meanwhile, the prince was flying ever higher on the magic horse. He soared through the clouds, toward the sun. Too late, he understood the trick that the Persian had played on him. He said, "There is no majesty or might save in Allah, the glorious and great! I am lost." But then, being a youth of wit and intelligence, he wondered whether, if there was a pin of ascent, there was not also a pin of descent, and eventually he found it on the left flank of the horse.

At once, the horse began to descend.

The prince was filled with exultation. Praising Allah, he began to turn the horse's head this way and that, riding the winds in joy and delight.

All day the prince put his magic steed through its paces in the cold, exhilarating air. Far below him he could see the cities and plains of unknown lands. Finally, tiring of the buffeting winds, he pulled the peg of descent, and landed on the terrace of a wonderful palace, in a strange, fair city.

Night fell, and the prince, leaving the ebony horse on the roof terrace, set off in search of food and drink. He descended a staircase to a courtyard paved with white marble and alabaster, glimmering in the moonlight. The whole palace was hushed and still.

At last, Prince Kamar al-Akmar saw a light flickering by the entrance to the harem. It was a lighted torch, and beside it was a slumbering servant. The prince helped himself to the sleeper's provisions and his sword, and, having eaten and drunk, ventured past him into the palace.

The prince drew aside a curtain, and behold! On a couch of whitest ivory lay a sleeping girl, covered in her own flowing tresses, like a new moon issued from the hand of the Creator. He approached her, trembling, and kissed her tenderly on the right cheek.

She opened her eyes, and asked him, "Who are you?"

"I am your slave," he replied.

"What brought you here?"

"My fate, and my fortune."

"Then," said the girl, whose name was Shams al-Nahar, "you must be the prince who asked for my hand in marriage yesterday, and whom my father rejected. He told me you were ugly, but he lied, for you are beautiful."

"I am not he," replied Kamar al-Akmar, "but I, too, would ask for your hand."

"And I would grant it," replied Shams al-Nahar, for her heart flamed with longing for this handsome stranger.

And they embraced.

The servant at the door of the harem, waking and discovering his sword gone and his food eaten, ran to the king. "Someone has broken into the harem, either man or jinni!"

The king drew his sword, and burst into his daughter's apartment. There he found Kamar al-Akmar, sleeping sweetly by her side. He bellowed with rage. The prince woke and, with an answering war cry, faced the king, sword in hand.

"Youth, are you a man or a jinni?" cried the king.

"If you were not my beloved's father," replied the prince, "you would die for that insult. I am a prince of the royal line of Persia."

"Prince or no, you have no business here."

"Why not?" said Kamar al-Akmar. "Where else would you find such a suitable match: rich, well-bred, courageous, handsome?"

"If you had come to me, after the custom of kings, and begged my daughter's hand in marriage, I would have welcomed you. But as you sneak into the harem behind my back, you must die."

"Let us fight if we must; but if I win, your throne is mine. Or, if that is not to your liking, I am willing to fight your entire army single-handed."

In the morning, the king summoned his entire army — forty thousand men — and drew them up in battle array. He said to them, "Soldiers, this upstart prince seeks my daughter's hand in marriage, and has offered to fight you all to win it. Let him feel your pikes and swords, to teach him some manners and humility."

Then the king turned to Prince Kamar al-Akmar and offered him the best horse in his stables, but the prince replied, "I want no other steed than the one on which I came here."

"And where is that?" asked the king.

"On the roof terrace," said the prince.

All who heard him sniggered, for no horse could ascend the stairs to reach the roof; but when they went to the terrace, they found the ebony horse waiting for its rider.

Prince Kamar al-Akmar mounted the horse, and pulled the pin of ascent. The horse bucked and swayed and then lifted itself into the air, soaring high, high above the futile pikes and swords of the troops. "Farewell," cried the prince, and his mocking laughter trailed behind him on the wind as he steered the ebony horse for home.

In the palace, the princess Shams al-Nahar lay weeping on her couch, lovelorn, inconsolable.

When Prince Kamar al-Akmar returned home on the ebony horse, he found the threshold strewn with the ashes of mourning, and his mother, father, and sisters clad in dreary black, for they thought him lost. When they saw him descend from the sky, their joy was even greater than their grief had been, and the king announced a holiday throughout the city.

"What is more," he declared, "I pardon everyone in my jails, whatever their crime. Open the doors and let them go free. All, that is, save that wicked Persian who made the horse."

"Forgive him, too, father," said the prince, "for the horse is truly wondrous."

So the Persian, too, was freed, but the king would not relent so far

as to grant him the hand of his youngest daughter, whom he promised instead to the handsome son of his grand wazir. Because of this, the sage seethed with vengeful feelings, and regretted ever allowing Prince Kamar al-Akmar to mount the magic horse and discover its secret.

That evening, at the celebration feast, a handmaiden played the lute and sang the company a song of parted lovers and broken hearts.

As he listened to her song, the prince felt the fires of longing flame in his heart. He arose, and went to the ebony horse. Ignoring his father's pleas, he mounted the horse, pulled the pin, and ascended once more into the air.

He flew all night until he came to the city of his beloved. Once more, he found the guard of the harem asleep, and entered. He found the princess sobbing, and took her by the hand. "Come," he said, and led her to the horse.

As they mounted the horse, the princess's father came onto the terrace. "Prince," he called, "do not take my daughter from me."

"My beloved," said the prince to the princess, "will you come with me, or shall I leave you with your parents?"

"I will come with you," said Shams al-Nahar, "for without you my heart can never be content."

So they rose into the air on the magic horse, and rode the winds back to Kamar al-Akmar's home. They landed in a quiet garden, outside the palace. The prince asked his beloved to wait there, while he went to find his father and announce the wonderful news that he had brought home a bride.

Alas! When the prince returned to the garden, with guards and handmaidens, jewels and garlands, drums and flutes, the princess was gone, and the horse, too.

Prince Kamar al-Akmar tore his clothes, beat his fists against his head, and ran raging and crying through the gardens.

He questioned the gardeners. "Has anyone come this way? Quick! The truth."

"No one, my lord, save the ancient Persian sage, who comes here to gather healing herbs."

And then the prince understood. The sage had taken back his horse, and stolen the princess, too.

"I will not rest until I have her back," he vowed.

Meanwhile, the ancient Persian had come across the princess and the ebony horse in the garden. He pretended that he was a messenger from the prince, sent to bring Shams al-Nahar to the palace. Although she found him ugly and frightening, the princess entrusted herself to him, thinking him a friend of her beloved. But when she joined him on the ebony horse, the sage flew away from the palace, not toward it.

"Where are you taking me?" cried the princess. "To the prince?"

"Allah may take pity on the prince, but I will not," replied the sage. "He is a mean, stingy knave, not fit to be the lowest of my servants."

"How dare you revile your master, and steal his magic steed?"

"He is not my master; I am yours. And the horse is mine. I constructed it, and I know all its secrets, as your paltry prince does not. Now that I have recovered it, I will sear his heart as he has seared mine. If I am not to have my princess, he will not have his. You will never see him again. You would do well to look to me for your protection, for I can be generous to those who please me."

The princess made no answer to this, but wept bitter tears.

They flew on, until they came to Greece. Here they descended into a meadow, to eat and drink. While they were there, the king of that land rode by and, noticing the ill-matched pair, called out, "Lady, what have you to do with this foul, loathsome old man?"

The Persian replied quickly, "Lord, this is my wife."

But the princess said, "This wicked man is no husband of mine. He has carried me off by fraud and force."

When he heard this, the king of Greece ordered the sage to be carried off to jail, while he asked the princess to accompany him back to the palace. He ordered his servants to bring the ebony horse, too, although he did not understand its virtue.

Far away, Prince Kamar al-Akmar was searching through all the lands, asking everywhere for news of the ebony horse; but no one had seen such a thing, and many pitied him, saying, "The fellow is stark, staring mad."

At last, however, he came to the land of the Greeks, and there he heard the story of how the king had found a beautiful princess in the company of a vile old man, and a wonderful ebony horse. He discovered that the Persian was in the dungeons, the ebony horse was in the royal treasure-house, and the princess Shams al-Nahar was in the palace. The king of Greece had fallen in love with her — who could not? — but she appeared to have lost her reason, and to now be quite insane. The king was desperate, and had offered any reward to the man who could cure her.

Therefore, the prince presented himself at the palace in the guise of a doctor, claiming to be able to cure any illness, but especially troubles of the mind. He was taken to see the princess, and found her tearing her hair and writhing on the ground. The prince, seeing immediately that this was a feigned madness, made a show of examining her, muttering nonsense words, and performing all sorts of mumbo jumbo, while whispering under his breath, "Do not fear. It is I, Kamar al-Akmar. I will rescue you."

He said to the king, "She is possessed by a jinni." He asked the king to describe again how he had found her in the meadow. "Ah!" he said. "No doubt the jinni's true body is the ebony horse. Let us go back to the meadow, bringing the horse, and I will drive the jinni from the girl back into the horse."

They all returned to the meadow, and Kamar al-Akmar and Shams al-Nahar climbed aboard the ebony horse. The prince pulled the pin of ascent, and the horse once again rose into the air, leaving the king of Greece stranded on the ground, bewailing his fate and cursing the prince for stealing away his heart's delight. But he had no hope of catching Kamar al-Akmar, so had to content himself with visiting justice on the evil old Persian sage.

As for the prince and the princess, they rode the ebony horse back to Persia, where the king welcomed Shams al-Nahar as if she were his own daughter. They were married without delay, and lived happily for long years, until the Destroyer of Delights, the Sunderer, the Plunderer, came to them, as he comes to all.

"That is all very well," said King Shahryar, "but what happened to the wonderful horse? I would pay any money for such a treasure."

"The ebony horse," said Sheherazade, "was destroyed by Prince Kamar al-Akmar's father, to prevent the prince straying from home again. Or so the story tells."

"What a fool," said King Shahryar.

"A fool is a fool, and an ass is an ass," said Sheherazade, "and if you spare me till tomorrow night, I can tell you a tale to prove it." And that night she told King Shahryar the story of

THE ASS

ONE DAY, a fool who was leading an ass to market was spotted by some sharp-witted rogues, who decided to play a trick on him.

"I'll take that man's ass away from him, and he'll never even object," said one. He sneaked up behind the fool, untied the halter from the neck of the ass, and fastened it around his own neck. The simpleton never noticed a thing.

Once his friends had hidden the ass out of sight, the man in the halter pulled up sharp. Without looking around, the fool gave a tug on the rope, but the man in the halter dug in his heels.

The fool turned around with a curse on his lips, only to see, not an ass, but a man, looking up at him from the halter with big, pleading eyes.

"What is this?" cried the fool. "Where is my ass?"

"I am here," replied the man. "I am your ass. Listen, master, to my tale.

"As a youth I was a bad lot, always mixing with low company, and never respecting my parents as a man should. One day when I was drunk I even went so far as to strike my dear mother, and she called down the curse of Allah upon me, and I found myself transformed into an ass.

"You, master, bought me in the market, and a hard life I have had of it ever since. I have been a beast of burden. You have beaten me, and sworn at me in language I would be ashamed to repeat. I have had to accept everything, for I could not speak. All I could do was snort and bray. But now, miraculously, I have returned to my true form. My mother must have taken pity on me and begged for the curse to be lifted."

The poor fool was quite taken in, and could only splutter out apologies for the harsh treatment he had meted out to the ass. "Forgive me, I beg," he asked. "Allah is all powerful, and all merciful. There is no help save in Allah." And he undid the halter and let the man go.

A few days later, the fool went back to the market to buy himself a new ass. He was amazed to see for sale his old ass, as large as life. As he approached it, the animal brayed in welcome, but the fool still did not see how he had been taken in. He spoke into the ass's ear, "You wicked young man. I can see you must have been beating your mother again. Well, do not think that I will buy you a second time!"

There came a night when the lamp in King Shahryar's bedchamber guttered and went out, and refused to light again. "Take it away," shouted the angry king, "and bring one that works!"

"Let us hope that they bring the wonderful lamp that once belonged to Aladdin," said Sheherazade.

"What lamp is that?" asked the king.

So Sheherazade entertained him in the darkness with the story of

ALADDIN

I T IS said, O King of the Age, that there once lived a poor tailor in a certain city in China. This tailor had a son, called Aladdin.

Now Aladdin was a rascal. Everyone said, "He'll come to no good." When he was ten, his father took him into his tailor's shop to learn an honest trade, but Aladdin was always slipping off into the street to play, like the little guttersnipe he was. His father was so disappointed in him that he fell sick and died.

The mother, seeing that her husband was dead and her son was good for nothing, sold the shop, and set about supporting the family by spinning. And while she toiled day and night over her spinning wheel, Aladdin roamed the streets playing silly pranks and getting into all sorts of scrapes. He only came home for meals.

When Aladdin was fifteen, he was loafing about one of the poor quarters of the city, with a group of other young rogues, when he was noticed by a stranger, a Moor. This Moor studied the lad long and hard, muttering to himself, "This must be the one!" He took one of the other boys aside, and questioned him closely about Aladdin.

Then he approached Aladdin himself, saying, "My boy, aren't you Aladdin, the tailor's son?"

"Yes," said Aladdin, "but my father has been dead for years."

At this, the Moor burst into tears, and clutched Aladdin to him.

"What's the matter?" asked Aladdin.

"Should I not cry, when you tell me my brother is dead?" exclaimed the Moor, his voice trembling with some deep emotion. "But at least I have found you, my nephew, blood of my blood. I knew you at once, even among this group of lads." The Moor stopped speaking to wipe the tears from his cheeks.

"Now," said the Moor, "take me home to your poor mother. You run ahead and tell her the news. She will be pleased to see you, for truly it is said, 'A son is the lamp of a dark house.'"

He pulled ten gold pieces from his purse. "Take these to her, and tell her I am coming."

Aladdin ran straight home to his mother, shouting, "My uncle is coming! My uncle is coming!"

"What are you talking about?" said his mother, who was very surprised to see him home in the daytime. "Your father did have a brother, but he is dead."

"It's true! Look, he gave me these coins!"

"Well," said the mother, looking at the gold, "perhaps I did not know all your father's brothers."

Presently the Moor arrived, followed by a servant carrying food and drink and sweetmeats. "The blessings of Allah be upon you, wife of my brother," he cried. "Now, show me where my brother used to sit."

When he was shown the spot, he cast himself to his knees and began wailing and kissing the ground, moaning, "What is left for me, when you are gone, O my brother, O vein of my eye!"

He continued sobbing and lamenting, until Aladdin's mother, quite worried at this show of grief, said, "You will kill yourself with weeping!" Then he allowed himself to be coaxed from the floor.

"You must be wondering where I have come from," he said, "for we have never met before. Forty years ago, I left this country to travel the world, and finally settled in the country of Morocco. But one day I fell to thinking of my old home and my brother, of blessed memory, and decided to come back to see him. Alas! I was too late. But at least I have found my nephew, Aladdin. As soon as I saw him in the street, I knew him for my brother's son. Blood calls to blood. And is it not said, 'He does not die who leaves a son'?"

Then the Moor turned to Aladdin. "You have grown into a fine young man, I can see. Tell me, what trade have you learned? I am sure you must work hard to support your mother."

Aladdin could only hang his head in shame, while his mother burst out, "Work! He doesn't know the meaning of the word. He's an idle young ne'er-do-well, who never does a moment's work. I've a good mind to lock the door against him, for all he does is sponge off me, and I'm not as young as I used to be. I can't keep him forever."

"What's this?" exclaimed the Moor. "Nephew, a man walks a straight line, but a wastrel staggers along. Be a man. I will apprentice you to any trade you have a mind to."

Aladdin didn't like the sound of this at all, and maintained a sullen silence.

So the Moor said, "I can see that you do not wish to learn a trade. Very well, I will set you up as a merchant."

At this, Aladdin's eyes brightened, for he knew that merchants lived in luxury.

The next day, the Moor took Aladdin into the city, and bought him a fine new suit of clothes such as rich merchants wear. Then he said, "Let us leave the rest of our business till tomorrow. Come with me and we will walk in the gardens outside the city, where the merchants have their pavilions. You can choose the one that you like best."

So they left the city, and strolled through the pleasure gardens. Aladdin was amazed by their beauties, but each time he tried to sit down to enjoy the flowers and the rippling streams and fountains, the Moor told him, "Do not rest yet. The best is still to come."

They walked far from the city, into the bare hills, and Aladdin began to whine and complain. "My feet hurt," he said.

"Be patient," said the Moor. "We are nearly there."

At last they came to the appointed spot, to reach which the Moor had journeyed halfway across the world. It was a deserted valley at the foot of a mountain, filled only with the presence of God.

"Now we can rest," said the Moor, "and soon you will see the most wonderful garden of all."

"But there is nothing here," objected Aladdin.

"Be patient," said the Moor, "and soon you will bless the day you met me, for you will see a sight no other living man has seen."

When they had rested awhile, the Moor told Aladdin to gather sticks to make a fire. He muttered his spells over this, and soon it began to billow with smoke. As the fire took hold, and the Moor gabbled his magic words faster and faster, the very earth began to split asunder. It gaped open to reveal a marble slab with a copper ring fixed in its middle.

Aladdin gave a frightened cry and began to run away, but the Moor sprang after him and felled him with a blow. "Stop whining," he said. "I am your uncle, and I am trying to make a man of you. Listen to me.

"Beneath that marble slab lies a treasure, set there by a mighty enchantment, sealed with your name. It is for you that I have opened the earth with my spells, for only you, Aladdin, can fetch this treasure from its hiding place. Obey me, and you will be rich beyond the dreams of kings."

"Command me, Uncle," said Aladdin. "I will obey."

Aladdin listened closely as the Moor told him how to reach the

treasure and then gave him a ring, saying, "If you follow my instructions, this will protect you." Then he walked up to the marble slab, seized hold of the copper ring, and cried, "Open! Open for Aladdin son of Mustafa son of Ali!" And the slab moved aside, revealing a flight of steps leading downward into the earth.

Down and down Aladdin walked. First he came into a hall full of jars of liquid gold; then into a hall full of jars of gold dust; then into a hall full of jars of gold coins. Aladdin was careful not to touch any of these or to allow his robe to brush against them, for the Moor had told him that if he did, he would be instantly turned to stone.

Beyond the third hall, Aladdin came to a magnificent garden, full of trees heavy with fruit. He walked through this till he came to a little terrace, on which he found what he had come for: a little copper lamp, burning on a pedestal. He extinguished the lamp and hid it in his robe, as he had been told to do.

Then Aladdin began to retrace his steps, while his uncle's words drummed in his head: "You will be rich. You will be rich. You will be rich."

As he passed back through the garden, Aladdin reached out to pluck fruit from the trees, for he was both hungry and thirsty. But he found the fruit was hard and inedible, for in that enchanted garden, the fruits of the trees were precious stones: diamonds and pearls, rubies and emeralds, sapphires and jaspers. Every kind of jewel was hanging there, burning with magical radiance.

Aladdin did not know what the strange fruits were, but nevertheless he began to gather them, thinking they would make fine presents for his mother and his friends. He stuffed as many as he could into his belt and his pockets and his robe, till he was loaded down like a pack donkey. Nevertheless, he managed to stagger through the three halls without touching anything, and reached the stairs without being turned to stone.

He could hear the Moor calling from above, "Where is the lamp?"

"I have it here, in my robe," he replied.

"Quickly, give it to me!" cried the Moor.

"How can I?" asked Aladdin. "I'm so laden down with these pretty fruits, I can't get at it."

ALADDIN

"Fool, give me the lamp!" shouted the Moor.

"Wait till I get out, and then you can have it," said Aladdin.

But the Moor, suspecting treachery, bellowed, "Son of a dog, give me the lamp, or die!"

Aladdin retreated back into the cave, while the Moor stamped and swore and tore his beard.

The Moor saw all his careful plans brought to nothing by the disobedience of a mere boy. His magical powers had told him that only Aladdin son of Mustafa son of Ali could enter the treasure cave that contained the magic lamp, which he had long coveted, and that was why he had sought Aladdin out and pretended to be his uncle. He was the greatest of all magicians of his day, but now this guttersnipe was thwarting him. It was too much! He raised his arms and uttered a ritual curse. At his bidding, the chasm in the earth closed up, trapping Aladdin inside. "Stay in there, you miserable wretch," he shouted, "and glut your greedy appetite on your precious fruits!"

With that, the Moor departed, to set sail once more for Morocco. All his plans had gone wrong, and he cursed his ill luck all the way home. To Aladdin, trapped in a dark dungeon to starve, he did not pay another thought.

When Aladdin found himself trapped underground, he soon realized that the Moor was not really his uncle, but a wicked magician who had been playing him for a fool. But it was too late now. Aladdin sat and wept.

It was pitch-dark in the cave, but a ray of light did fall through one chink in the rock. It glinted on the ring that the Moor had given to Aladdin to help him in time of trouble. The Moor had forgotten all about the gift in his rage, as Aladdin had in his despair. But now Aladdin noticed the ring, and began to wonder about its uses.

Aladdin rubbed the ring with his fingers, and immediately a jinni appeared, bowing low and saying, "Hail, lord and master of the ring. Your servant awaits your commands."

"Take me up to the surface of the earth," said Aladdin.

Aladdin returned to the city and went to his mother's house,

weeping and shivering with hunger and terror. He told her all about his ordeal at the hands of his supposed uncle, the Moorish magician.

"That dog, that liar, that twister, that devil of all devils! He brought me face to face with death, and all for a paltry copper lamp." Aladdin fetched the lamp from his robes, and with it spilled some of the jewels he had gathered from the enchanted trees. "And to think that I in turn risked my life for these useless baubles," he said.

"Let us thank Allah that that wicked man's plot did not succeed," said Aladdin's mother. "I should have known by his bleary eyes that he was not your father's brother."

On the next day, Aladdin told his mother, "I see now that I have been an unworthy son to you. I will go out and seek work. But first I must eat, for I am weak with hunger."

"Alas," replied his mother, "there is no food in the house."

"In that case," said Aladdin, "let us take that copper lamp to the market, and see if anyone will give us a coin for it, to buy some bread."

Aladdin's mother picked up the lamp and, seeing that it was dirty, began to polish it, thinking that it might fetch a better price if it was clean. As she rubbed, a terrifying jinni surged out of thin air toward her, his vast head scraping against the ceiling. It bowed to her, and its voice boomed out, "I am master of earth and air and wave, but slave of the lamp, and the bearer's slave. Your will commands me, mistress, whatever you crave."

Aladdin's mother shrieked and fell to the floor in a faint.

Aladdin, who had already mastered the jinni of the ring, plucked the lamp from his mother's limp hand, and said, "Jinni, I am hungry. Fetch me a feast." And the jinni did as he asked.

Aladdin roused his mother with rose water. "Wake up, mother, and do not be afraid. See what the jinni has brought us! Come and eat, before the food gets cold."

But his mother said, "The food would stick in my throat. For this jinni is an evil thing, and no good can come from it. I beg you, my son, to throw away that lamp, and the ring as well."

"Anything but that," said Aladdin. "But if it offends you, I will keep the lamp hidden."

Although Aladdin would not throw away the lamp, he did not want to use it again too soon and risk another encounter with the jinni. So for some years he and his mother lived by selling the gold plates on which the jinni had brought the feast, and using the proceeds to buy food. In visiting the jewel merchants to sell the plates, Aladdin noticed in their shops many strange fruits like those that he had brought back from the cave, though smaller and less sparkling than his, and soon learned the value of his haul, which he locked up with the lamp.

Now it happened one day that Aladdin was talking to one of the jewel merchants when he heard the king's crier calling, "By command of our magnificent master, the King of the Time and the Lord of the Age and the Tide, let all retire indoors. For the lady Badr al-Budur, the beauteous daughter of the king, will pass along this street, and must not be looked on, on pain of death."

When Aladdin heard this, he was seized with a longing to see the princess, and hid himself behind a door where he could look out into the street. And so it was that he saw passing the lovely princess Badr al-Budur. It was as if his eyes were blinded by the sun. The blood ran hot in his veins; his legs buckled beneath him.

He walked home to his mother like one in a dream. "I will not rest,"
he said, "until I have won the princess for my bride."

"Do not talk so foolishly," said his mother. "You are but a poor
orphan, the son of a tailor. The princess must marry some great lord."

"Nevertheless," said Aladdin, "I must have her."

He went to his locked chest and took out the jewels he had carried
from the enchanted cave. "If you love me, Mother, you will take these
to the sultan as my gift, and beg him for his daughter's hand."

So Aladdin's mother went to the palace, and asked to see the king.
Now the king held court every day, and anyone who had some
problem or grievance could take it to him for advice or judgment.
There was always a great throng of people, each one more eager than

the last to be heard. Aladdin's mother was quite overwhelmed, and just sat, shy and silent, till it was time to go.

This went on for days. She never quite summoned up the courage to speak, and Aladdin nearly went mad with waiting. But at last the king himself noticed the shabby old woman who came every day and just sat clutching something wrapped in a shawl, never daring to speak. "Who is that woman?" he asked.

His wazir replied, "It is just a foolish old crone. Probably someone has sold her rotten barley, or some such foolishness."

But the king said, "Bring her to me."

When Aladdin's mother was brought before the king, she prostrated herself on the ground before him.

89

"Tell me," he said, "why do you come here every day, and never speak?"

"First of all, O Lord of the Age, please forgive me beforehand for what I am about to ask. I could not speak if I thought you would be angry with me."

"I will not be angry," said the king. "Now, come to the point."

"The point is," said Aladdin's mother, "my boy Aladdin wants to marry your daughter."

The whole court rocked with laughter at this; the king himself wept tears of mirth. Wiping his eyes, he asked, "And what dowry would he bring?"

Silently, Aladdin's mother unwrapped her shawl and let the fiery jewels spill across the floor.

The king picked up some of the jewels, and gazed at them in wonder. "Here is beauty indeed," he exclaimed. "I never dreamed of seeing stones as fine as these."

"How could you have?" said the wazir. "For the smallest of these stones is worth the whole of your treasury."

"In that case," said the king, "do you not think that young Aladdin, this worthy woman's son, who has sent me this gift, is a proper match for the princess Badr al-Budur?"

"Y-y-yes, my lord," stammered the wazir, "but remember, O Lord of the Age, that the princess is already promised in marriage to my own son. In fairness, I ask you to allow me three months to find a dowry even grander than Aladdin's."

The king knew that no one could match Aladdin's jewels, but he consented to the three months' delay, not wishing to offend the wazir.

Aladdin's mother hastened home with the good news. "The king has agreed to the marriage," she said. "But there is to be a delay of three months, to allow the wazir to match your dowry. I wouldn't trust that wazir as far as I could throw him, but even in three months there is surely nothing he can do to prevent the match."

"We must just be patient," answered Aladdin.

Agonizingly slowly, the days crawled by.

When two of the three months had passed, Aladdin's mother happened to go into the market one day to buy provisions. She noticed that all the shops were decorated with bright flags and hung with lanterns, and that everybody was dressed as if for a holiday. She asked a merchant what was going on.

"You must be a stranger here," he replied, "not to know that today is the wedding day of the Princess Badr al-Budur. She is marrying the son of the wazir."

When Aladdin heard the news, he felt he had been struck by a thunderbolt. All his dreams withered away. He had given away his jewels, and lost his princess. But then he remembered that he still had the lamp.

He took the lamp from its hiding place and summoned the jinni. It appeared, as ferocious-looking as ever, bellowing, "I am master of earth and air and wave, but slave of the lamp, and the bearer's slave. Your will commands me, whatever you crave."

Aladdin said, "Tonight the Princess Badr al-Budur, my promised bride, is to marry the son of the treacherous wazir. When they retire to bed, transport the bed here, with them inside it."

"It shall be done," said the jinni.

No sooner were the bride and bridegroom in bed, than they were lifted in the twinkling of an eye from their room in the palace into Aladdin's room. Aladdin took one look at the wazir's son, trembling and whimpering on the bed, and motioned to the jinni. "Take that lily-livered lout and throw him into a stinking ditch for the night."

And so Aladdin was left alone with the princess Badr al-Budur, his heart's delight. "Have no fear, princess," he said, "I mean you no harm. Your father has promised you in marriage to me and accepted my marriage gift; therefore this evil-hearted wazir and his sneak of a son have no claim on you. Rest easy: all will be well." And with that, Aladdin settled himself beside the princess on the bed, but with a naked sword lying between them.

Aladdin soon fell into a happy sleep, but the poor princess never got a wink. As for the wazir's son, every time he crawled out of the foul ditch into which he had been thrown, the jinni pushed him back in.

In the morning, the wazir's son staggered back into the house very much the worse for wear, with slime and filth smeared all over him. As soon as he arrived, Aladdin said, "Slave of the lamp, return them to the palace."

And so it was that when the king and queen went up in the morning to see the married couple, they found Badr al-Budur weeping and the wazir's son desperately trying to scrub himself clean.

"What's this?" asked the king. "What's going on?"

"Oh, Mother," cried the princess, "it was terrible!" And she told her mother and father all that had happened.

The king turned to the wazir's son. "What sort of a man do you call yourself, to allow your bride to be abducted on her wedding night, and never lift a finger to protect her? I declare the marriage annulled. You are not fit to be her husband."

"Allah be praised!" said the wazir's son. "Another night in the ditch would have finished me off."

That day, Aladdin himself arrived at the palace, dressed in the height of magnificence, like a conquering prince. His servants, conjured by the jinni, were carrying forty gold dishes heaped with glowing jewels. Aladdin himself was riding the proudest purebred stallion ever seen. The air was alive with music and cheering, and crowds lined the streets to watch him go by.

"Welcome!" said the king, thinking that this guest must be some visiting royalty. "Tell me, from what country have you come, and what is your lineage?"

"Why," said Aladdin, "I come from this very city, and my name is Aladdin son of Mustafa son of Ali. My father was a tailor, but I have never followed the trade, having wealth enough to live a simple modest life." With that, Aladdin beckoned forward the servants, who began to pour jewels without measure at the king's feet. "Please," said Aladdin, "accept this small token of my loyalty, and of my devotion to your daughter, the princess Badr al-Budur."

The king saw that there was nothing for it but to swallow his pride. He replied, "I welcome you to my family, Aladdin. No father could hope for a better match for his daughter, even if you are the son of a tailor. Let us arrange the wedding at once."

"No," said Aladdin. "First I must build a magnificent palace, fit for

your daughter to live in. In order to do so, I beg you to give me the land next-door to your palace."

"By all means," said the king. "But remember, this palace has taken generations to build. I do not see how you can erect anything as grand in your lifetime, however rich you are."

"Nevertheless," said Aladdin, "it shall be done."

Back at home, Aladdin summoned the jinni once more, and ordered it to build a palace worthy of the princess on the open land next to the king's dwelling.

By next morning, it was done. The palace was as Aladdin had ordered in every detail. It was made entirely of rare and costly materials, and at its middle was a graceful crystal dome, supported by columns of gold and silver, pierced by ninety-nine windows. Ninety-eight of the windows were encrusted with diamonds, rubies, and emeralds, but the ninety-ninth was left unfinished.

The king was astonished, when he looked out from his own palace, to see what had been achieved in the course of a single night.

His wazir told him, "No good will come of this. This man Aladdin — a mere tailor's son, as we know — must be a magician, trafficking with dark powers, to do such a thing."

But the king answered, "You are just jealous. Aladdin is a rich and powerful man, quite capable of ordering a palace to be built between dusk and dawn of a single night. And look: One of the windows is unfinished. Surely a palace built by magic would be perfect in every particular. The unfinished window shows that even Aladdin ran out of time."

And so Aladdin and Badr al-Budur were married, and for some years lived happily in Aladdin's magnificent new palace, next-door to the princess's old home.

Aladdin did not let his riches go to his head and cause him to grow puffed up and proud. Instead, he remembered his childhood among the poor, and gave generously to all who needed help, especially widows like his mother, who had been left to bring up children on their own. His own mother came to live in the new palace and be a companion to Badr al-Budur when Aladdin was out hunting or attending to the duties of a prince.

Now in all this time, Aladdin had given no further thought to the wicked Moor who had trapped him underground, pretending to be his uncle. But the Moor remembered Aladdin well, for not an hour passed in which he did not curse Aladdin's name and mourn the loss of the magic lamp, which would have made him the richest and most powerful man in the world.

One day the Moor, musing on his ill fortune, began to wonder whether, even if Aladdin had died in the cave, there might not be some other way to win the lamp. So he cast his spells once again, to find out what he could. When his magic powers told him that not only was Aladdin still alive, but in possession of the lamp, and married to the king's daughter, he was beside himself with fury. He spat and screamed and foamed at the mouth, yelling, "Son of a dog, I spit in your face! Foul gallows bird, I will dance on your grave!"

The Moor lost no time in returning to China. There it seemed to him that people could talk of nothing else but "Prince Aladdin": how noble and brave and generous and wonderful in every respect was Prince Aladdin. The Moor muttered into his beard, "If I have my way, soon these hounds will be baying for Aladdin's blood and denouncing him as the good-for-nothing son of a tailor."

Hearing that Aladdin had gone hunting, and was not expected home for several days, the Moor hatched a plan. First he went to a coppersmith and bought a dozen cheap new copper lamps. Then, with his lamps in a basket, he walked up and down outside Aladdin's palace, crying in a loud voice, "New lamps for old! New lamps for old!"

Princess Badr al-Budur flung open a window to hear what was going on. Seeing the Moor walking up and down, followed by a gaggle of jeering children, and making his mad offer of "New lamps for old," she couldn't help laughing. And because Aladdin had never told her the secret of the magic lamp, she thought of the old lamp he kept in his chambers, and decided to send a servant out to see if the Moor really would exchange it. She thought it would be a wonderful surprise for Aladdin when he came home, to find his battered old lamp replaced by a brand-new one. As Aladdin seemed to have endless riches, it was always hard to think of little gifts to please him.

A servant took the lamp out to the Moor, who, when he saw the

lamp finally within his grasp, began to tremble and shake. The servant asked, "Is something wrong? Is the lamp too old?"

"No," said the Moor. "Give me the lamp, and take a new one."

The Moor took the lamp to a secluded place, and, his breath in his mouth, rubbed it. The jinni swelled into being, booming as always, "I am master of earth and air and wave, but slave of the lamp, and the bearer's slave. Your will commands me, whatever you crave." For the jinni truly was the slave of the lamp and whoever possessed it, be they good or evil.

The Moor said, "Slave of the lamp, I order you to transport me, together with the palace of Aladdin and everyone in it, to Morocco."

And the jinni replied, "Close your eyes, and open them again, and you will be in Morocco, in Aladdin's palace."

When the king woke that morning, he opened his window to see — nothing. Where Aladdin's palace had stood was bare ground.

He called for his wazir.

"Quickly, man," he shouted, "tell me what has happened to my daughter."

"What do you mean?" asked the wazir.

"Look! Look!" shrieked the king, pointing out the window. "The palace has gone, and taken Princess Badr al-Budur with it."

Then the wazir saw his chance. "Far be it from me to say 'I told you so,' Your Majesty, but I did warn you that Aladdin must have built that palace by magic. And is it not a proverb, 'What is brought by the wind will be carried away by the wind'?"

"Aladdin will die for this," answered the king grimly. "When he returns from the hunt, have him dragged to me in chains, like the treacherous dog he is."

The king did not even ask Aladdin for an explanation, and condemned him to death at once. But when the people heard that Aladdin was to die, they began to scale the walls of the palace to rescue him, and the king and the wazir did not dare to carry out the sentence.

Instead, the king told Aladdin that he would pardon him, but only so that he could search for the princess; if ever he came back without her, his life was forfeit.

Aladdin was sorely puzzled by the disappearance of his palace, but he remembered that he had carelessly left the lamp out in his room, and not locked away as usual, and guessed that something terrible must have happened.

He went down to the river and wrung his hands in grief and fear. And, as once before in time of trial, he rubbed the ring that the Moor had given him, when he was only a boy. The jinni of the ring appeared, and Aladdin said, "Jinni, I beg you, bring back my palace and my wife."

"That I cannot do," said the jinni, "for I cannot meddle with the work of the jinni of the lamp."

"In that case," said Aladdin, "take me, and set me down below the windows of my wife, Princess Badr al-Budur."

The princess spied him from her window and, as the Moor was not present, beckoned him into the palace. Then she told him how the Moor had tricked her into giving away the magic lamp, which the Moor now carried with him everywhere, boasting of its powers.

"That wicked magician told me you had been executed by my father. He seeks to marry me. If he finds you here, my love, he will kill you."

"Do not worry," said Aladdin, "for I have this ring, which, while it is not as powerful as the lamp, will help us overcome this tyrant, who is not fit to possess such a treasure."

Aladdin rubbed the ring, and the jinni appeared. "Fetch me a sleeping drug," he said, "strong enough to kill an elephant." And the jinni did so.

Then Aladdin turned to the princess. "Tonight," he said, "when the Moor comes to you with his loathsome courtship, speak kindly to him. Offer him a cup of wine, with this drug dissolved in it. He will drink it, and I will take back the lamp."

It happened just as Aladdin planned. Princess Badr al-Budur welcomed the Moor into her room with smiles and downcast glances, and begged him to drink with her. The Moor was too enthralled by her beauty to notice the powder in the wine and, as soon as he had drunk it down, he fell senseless to the floor.

Aladdin, who had been hiding behind a screen, leaped forward and seized the lamp.

The jinni came once more to Aladdin's summons, calling, "I am master of earth and air and wave, but slave of the lamp, and the bearer's slave. Your will commands me, whatever you crave."

"Deal with this vile magician so that he can do no more evil, and then take us back home," said Aladdin.

"And as far as I know," said Sheherazade, "Aladdin and Badr al-Budur lived happily ever after."

"But what happened to the lamp?" asked King Shahryar. "A man could use such a thing."

"The lamp, O light of my darkness," she answered, "the lamp is lost."

And on another night, Sheherazade told King Shahryar the story of

THE SPEAKING BIRD, THE SINGING TREE, AND THE GOLDEN WATER

THERE WAS once, long ago, a king of Persia named Khusrau Shah. He was so just a ruler that in his day even the tiger and the lamb drank from the same stream.

Not only was Khusrau Shah just, he was also wise. He knew that no king can trust the flatterers and schemers of his court to tell him the truth, but that he can always trust the common people. Therefore it was the practice of Khusrau Shah to disguise himself as a merchant and, together with his wazir, walk unnoticed at night through the streets of the city, to see what was to be seen and hear what was to be heard.

One night the shah and his wazir were strolling in the poorest quarter of the city when they heard women's voices coming from the humblest house in the street. The shah squinted through a crack in the door, and saw three young sisters sitting and chatting after their evening meal. They were discussing their hearts' desires.

The eldest said, "I wish I were married to the shah's head baker. I could eat pastries all day, and then how you would envy my curves and my delicate complexion!"

The second said, "The shah's cook is the man for me. For then I could eat every day those spiced dishes that I love. Just to think of the baked stuffed cucumbers makes my mouth water."

The third, who was the prettiest of them all, said nothing, and her sisters asked her, "Why so silent? If you don't make a choice, we'll have to marry you to the shah's groom, and send you off to live in the stables!"

99

The two sisters collapsed in giggles at this, but the youngest sister merely replied, "I would marry no one but our shah himself. I would bear him princes, handsome, brave, and just. And I would bear him a princess as pretty as the sky's smile. Her hair would be of silver and gold, her tears would be falling pearls, and her laughter would be coins of gold; her smile would be the smile of a budding rose."

The shah was amazed at what he had heard. At first he laughed, but, beneath his laughter, he found in his heart the desire to grant the wishes of the three sisters. So, next day, he sent the wazir to bring them to court.

They came before him trembling, but he told them, "Do not worry. Today is your day of destiny. Nothing is hidden from kings, and I know the secret desires of your hearts. You" — he turned to the eldest — "will be married today to my baker. And you" — he turned to the middle one — "will be married to my cook." Lastly he looked into the eyes of the youngest sister. "You, my dear, I will marry myself, and you will be my queen."

And so it came about. But while the youngest sister was blissfully happy with her choice, the two older sisters could not be content. Although they had their hearts' desires, when they saw how grand their sister had become, they grew full of spite and envy. Whenever they met, they could talk of nothing but how unjust and wrong it was that their younger sister should have become a queen, while they had married only a cook and a baker. They were quite eaten up with bitterness.

After nine months, by the grace of Allah, the queen gave birth to a son: a perfect prince, as fair as the crescent of a new moon. But the queen, in her innocence, had asked for her two sisters to be her midwives. They saw the chance to break her heart, and seized it.

As soon as the child was born, the sisters took it and, placing it in a willow basket, set it adrift on the canal that washed against the palace walls. Then they put in its place a little dead puppy.

Wailing, they called for the other women of the palace to come and see the horrible thing to which the queen had given birth.

When the shah was told what had happened, the world grew dark in his eyes.

As for the little baby prince, destiny decreed that, as his basket bobbed along in the water, it caught the eye of the shah's gardener. He fetched the basket to the bank with a stick, and found inside the perfect baby boy.

Now, the gardener and his wife had no children, though they had always wanted them. So they accepted the baby as the gift of Allah, and brought it up as their own.

In the following year, the queen gave birth to a second son, as fair as the first. But her wicked sisters repeated their cruel trick, setting the child adrift and replacing it with a dead kitten. But once more, the baby was rescued and adopted by the gardener and his wife.

In the year after that, the queen gave birth to a daughter. Yet again, the sisters cast away the baby, and for a third time it was found and taken in by the gardener. This time, the sisters replaced the baby with a dead muskrat.

The shah could bear it no longer. "The queen must herself be a monster, to give birth to such creatures," he said. "Therefore, let her be put into a wooden cage beside the mosque, and when the faithful go to prayer, each one shall spit in her face as he passes."

And so, at last, the two wicked sisters were able to enjoy their husbands' pastries and spiced dishes with light and merry hearts, thinking of their sister's shame and misery.

The days and years pass for the innocent and guilty alike: for the poor queen, caged like a wild beast; for her sisters, gloating in idleness; and for the three children, brought up with love and kindness by the gardener and his wife.

The two boys were Farid and Faruz, and the girl was Farizad. She was as beautiful as her mother had promised, and so was called Farizad of the Rose's Smile.

The children grew up handsome, brave, and wise. They studied the arts and the sciences. They learned to read and write, and to play musical instruments. They learned to hunt, and to hurl the javelin and shoot with the bow.

But as the children grew up, so the gardener and his wife grew old. Eventually, the gardener begged the shah to let him retire, and the shah, in gratitude for so many years' loyal service, gave him a mansion to live in, with a magnificent garden, laid out by the old man himself. There the family lived for several years in peace and happiness, until first the gardener's wife and then the gardener himself passed, as all must, into the mercy of Allah.

Farid and Faruz and Farizad stayed on in the house, knowing nothing of the secret of their birth, and wanting nothing more than the happy life they knew. The two brothers often went out hunting in the far country, but their sister usually preferred to wander in the perfect gardens, with their high walls, scented flowers, restful streams, and flocks of calling birds.

Now one day when Farid and Faruz were out, the servant told Farizad that an old woman had come to the gate, begging. Farizad, who had been taught to respect the old and show charity to the poor, asked the old woman into the garden, and fetched her all sorts of good things to eat.

When they had enjoyed the garden for a while, Farizad asked the old woman what she thought of it. "Well," said the old woman. "It is certainly an enchanting spot. I have wandered over the length and breadth of Allah's world, and I have never rested in a more beautiful garden. Indeed, there are only three things I can think of that would improve it."

"What are they?" asked Farizad.

"The first is the Speaking Bird, Bulbul al-Hazar. Rarest of all the birds, his song is so enticing that all the other birds flock to join him. The second is the Singing Tree. When its leaves are caressed by the wind, its harmonies are more beautiful than the lute or harp. And the

third is the Golden Water. The waters of your garden would cease to run, in admiration of that water. A single drop of it, let fall into an empty basin, will spout upwards in a jet of golden spray, rising, falling, never overflowing. The Speaking Bird would ease his throat drinking that water; the Singing Tree would refresh the thousand invisible mouths of its leaves with the spray.

"If these three things were in your garden, O Rose's Smile, your beauty would have found its true setting."

"Where can these things be found?" asked Farizad.

"The road starts here," said the old woman. "Whoever seeks these things must travel east for twenty days, and, on the twentieth day, ask the first man he meets, 'Where are the Speaking Bird, the Singing Tree, and the Golden Water?' The seeker will be directed to them."

After the old woman had gone, Farizad walked once more in the fragrant alleys of her garden. But somehow its charm was gone. It seemed dull and boring without the wonders of which the old woman had told her.

When Farid and Faruz returned from hunting, they traced Farizad to a hidden corner of the garden, by following the trail of pearls that were her tears.

"What is the matter, Rose's Smile?" they asked.

"I can no longer enjoy our father's garden," she answered, "for I have heard of three wondrous things that I long to have. Without them, I cannot be happy." And she told her brothers what the old woman had told her.

Farid said, "This is no great matter. I will seek these things and bring them to you." He drew his hunting knife, the handle of which was crusted with the pearls of Farizad's first baby tears. "Keep this in your care, brother and sister. If you look at it, you will get news of me. As long as the blade is clean and bright, you will know I am well and safe. If it grows dull and rusty, you will know that I am ill or in trouble. If it becomes stained with blood, you will know I am dead." And with that he rode off to the east on his journey.

On the twentieth day, Farid came to a meadow in which he found an old holy man sitting beneath a tree. This man had been so long withdrawn from the world that his beard had grown so thick and tangled that, when he replied to Farid's greeting, only a mumble could be heard.

"O holy one," said Farid, taking a pair of scissors from his pack, "allow me to attend to your beard, which, in your years of meditation, has grown to be more like that of a bear than that of a man." Taking the old man's mumble to be a yes, Farid began to clip away, trimming the beard, eyebrows, and hair of the holy man, and cutting twenty years of growth from his fingernails.

When the old man felt himself released from the burden of all this useless growth, he smiled at Farid and said, "Son, how may I help you?"

"Tell me where I will find the Speaking Bird, the Singing Tree, and the Golden Water," answered Farid. "I have come far, seeking them."

The old man fell silent, and would not reply.

"Do you not know the way?" asked Farid.

"I know the way," said the holy man, "but I do not wish to set you on it. For many and many a young man has passed that way before you, and never a one has returned."

"I do not care about danger," answered Farid. "Tell me the way."

The old man took a red ball from his pouch and gave it to Farid, saying, "Throw this ball in front of you. As long as it rolls, ride after it,

but when it comes to a halt, at the foot of a hill, dismount from your horse, and leave him; he will wait for your return.

"You must climb the hill on foot. On every side you will see scattered black rocks; these are what remains of the other young men who have dared this ascent. For as you climb, you will hear a chorus of voices — some urging you on, some mocking, some threatening you with vile torments. These are the voices of unseen demons. They will freeze your blood. And if you lose heart, or once look back, they will turn you to stone like the others.

"If you can withstand the demon voices, you will find Bulbul al-Hazar, the Speaking Bird, in a cage at the top of the hill. Speak, and he will answer you. Allah go with you."

Farid followed the ball to the foot of the hill, dismounted, and began to climb, as the old man had told him. At once the air was full of voices, whistling, shrieking, moaning, calling, wheedling, cursing. Farid bore it all, until one terrible voice, screaming right into his face, caused him to quail and look aside. At once he was turned into a block of black, unfeeling stone.

That night, when Farizad checked the hunting knife that Farid had left with her, she found that it was dull and flecked with rust. She called for Faruz, and they considered what they should do. "This is all my fault," said Farizad, "for setting my heart on those wondrous things the old woman told me about, instead of being content with what I had."

"What will be, will be," answered Faruz. "I will find our brother, and together we will win the Speaking Bird, the Singing Tree, and the Golden Water."

Before he left, Faruz gave his sister a necklace of pearls, strung from the tears of her girlhood. "If the pearls move freely on the string," he said, "you will know all is well with me. If they stick together, then you will know that Farid's fate has overtaken me also."

And, indeed, it happened with Faruz exactly as with Farid. He had climbed nearly to the top of the hill when he seemed to hear his brother's despairing voice crying, "Brother, do not pass me by!" He turned to look, and was transformed instantly to stone.

When, on the twentieth day after his departure, Farizad began to feel the pearls sticking together, she wept new pearls, more shining and perfect than ever before.

But Farizad was a girl of spirit and bravery. She dressed herself in men's clothes, mounted her horse, and set off after her beloved brothers.

On the twentieth day, Farizad came to the holy man. She asked him, "Father, have you seen two handsome young men who rode this way seeking the Speaking Bird, the Singing Tree, and the Golden Water?"

"You must be Farizad of the Rose's Smile," replied the old man, who, careless of the present, saw both past and future. "Indeed I saw both your brothers, and directed them to follow the ball, and climb the hill to find what they sought. But I fear they have been vanquished by the voices of the invisible demons who haunt the mountain where these treasures are to be found, and have been turned to stone like so many before them.

"Those demons cannot be seen by mortal eye, nor pierced by blade or arrow. But they can be defeated by a king's daughter and a wisp of cotton. Bend down your head, Farizad!"

Farizad bent down her head, her glorious gold and silver hair hanging free. The holy man took a wisp of cotton from his pouch, divided it into two parts, and tucked these in Farizad's ears.

Farizad followed the ball to the hill, dismounted, and began to climb. All around, the invisible demons howled and screeched, in a hideous hubbub of shrieks, groans, and moans. But to Farizad, her ears cushioned by the cotton, this vile cacophony seemed but the muffled noise of a distant crowd. "Mock on, spirits, mock on!" she cried. "I do not fear or heed you!"

As she approached the top of the hill, the noise grew so terrifying that the bravest of heroes would have thrown himself to his knees and begged for mercy; but Farizad trudged on, uncaring, unafraid. When she reached the summit, she saw, in a gold cage on a gold pedestal, Bulbul al-Hazar, the Speaking Bird. The distant roaring of the invisible spirits stilled; the demons, thwarted, slept.

Farizad took the cotton from her ears, and laid hold of the golden cage, saying, "I have you, bird! You shall never escape me!"

The bird fluted a reply:

> *"Farizad, Rose's Smile,*
> *Brighter than moon or star,*
> *I will serve you for a while,*
> *For I know just who you are."*

So Farizad asked Bulbul al-Hazar, the Speaking Bird, where she could find the Singing Tree and the Golden Water. He sang to her where they were, and what to do, and soon she had broken off a little branch of the Singing Tree, while the wind played gentle melodies among its leaves, and filled a crystal flagon with the Golden Water, which gushed in a stream of liquid gold from a wall of turquoise.

Then Farizad said, "O Bulbul al-Hazar, thank you for helping me to find the Singing Tree and the Golden Water. But my most important task is still to do. How may I free my brothers, and the other brave souls, from their imprisonment in these slabs of rock on the hillside?"

The Speaking Bird replied:

> *"Nothing can help them, save alone,*
> *Golden water on black stone."*

So Farizad sprinkled some drops of water on each of the stones, and as soon as she had done so, the stone took human shape, and a fair young man rose from the ground, stretching and sighing like one roused from the depths of sleep. The first two to revive were Farid and Faruz, for they were the bravest and had climbed the farthest. Soon there was a whole troop of young adventurers, surprised back into life on the sunlit hillside.

A merry journey they made of it back into the meadow and westward to their homes. They stopped to speak once again to the old holy man, but he had gone. His long vigil by that hill of demons was over, now that Farizad had quelled the voices, with the help of a wisp of cotton and a true heart. One by one, the young men whom Farizad had rescued branched off from the road to seek their own homes, till at last there were left only Farid, Faruz, and Farizad of the Rose's Smile.

As soon as they arrived home, Farizad hung the Speaking Bird in his gold cage in a bower of jasmine. At once he began to sing, and all the birds of the garden flocked to his side, to blend their voices with his in praise and joy.

Then Farizad went to a fountain of alabaster, and let fall into it one drop of the golden water. The bead of gold sprayed up from the urn in a shower of glory — rising, falling, never overflowing — in the sun-flecked air.

And finally Farizad planted the branch of the Singing Tree, and watched in wonder as it took root and grew, within moments, into a magnificent tree, among whose boughs the wind began to play its unceasing melodies.

Once more, Farid and Faruz and Farizad were happy in their enchanted garden, living each day for its own pleasure, and wanting nothing more. Seeing Farizad so content, Farid and Faruz began once more to ride out hunting, and so it was they met one day great Khusrau Shah.

They introduced themselves to their king as the sons of his old gardener, and asked him to grace their house with his presence. The king was charmed by the two young men, who stood so straight and tall and spoke with such modest confidence, so he agreed to visit them the following day.

When Farizad heard that the shah himself was coming to visit, she did not know what to do. She consulted Bulbul al-Hazar, the Speaking Bird, whose advice she had come to trust in all things. Bulbul replied:

> *"Your fate approaches from afar;*
> *Now at last, the tale unfurls.*
> *Prepare no feast for Khusrau Shah:*
> *Feed him cucumbers, stuffed with pearls."*

"Surely you mean rice, not pearls," said Farizad.

But the Speaking Bird just repeated the last words of its song, trilling, *"with pearls, with pearls, with pearls."*

As there was a plentiful store of pearls in the house, from the days of Farizad's sadness, Farizad ordered the dish to be prepared.

When the shah arrived, Farid and Faruz led him into the garden, and introduced him to Farizad, who, following Bulbul's advice, was veiled, for the first time in her life. Even so, the shah was quite overcome with her grace and purity. He began to tremble with emotion, to think that his old gardener had been blessed with three such perfect children, while he had only met with misery and shame.

But when they showed him the Golden Water — rising, falling, never overflowing — he exclaimed with delight, for its serene rain seemed to cool the mind.

Then he heard the music of the Singing Tree, issuing forth on the wind as if from nowhere, and it seemed to sing of comfort, like the music of dreams.

The shah exclaimed, "This is a house of peace. In such a place I could cast aside my power, and my sorrow, and live in simple happiness."

"You have not yet seen the crowning glory of the garden," said Farid. "Come with us to the jasmine bower, and we shall eat stuffed cucumbers at the side of Bulbul al-Hazar, the Speaking Bird."

As they rested, breathing in the sweet smell of jasmine, the servant brought out the dishes of stuffed cucumbers, and the shah said, "These look perfect; even better than those prepared by my own cook." But when he took the first mouthful, he soon discovered that, instead of rice or nuts, they were stuffed with pearls. "What is the meaning of this?" he demanded.

And Bulbul al-Hazar, the Speaking Bird, replied:

"The dish is strange, but stranger still
Is a king who questions Allah's will.
You, who once were called 'the Just,'
Have forfeited your people's trust.
Your queen is caged as if a beast,
While her sisters gloat and feast.
Behold! O shah, your sons and daughter,
By the Speaking Bird, the Singing Tree, and the Golden Water."

The shah's eyes were opened; blood spoke to blood. He embraced his sons, Farid and Faruz, crying, "My sons!" He gazed on his daughter, Farizad. She unveiled, and he saw that her hair was gold and silver, and that her smile was, indeed, like a budding rose. She shed a tear of joy, and it fell to the ground as a pearl; she laughed with joy, and her laughter was gold coins. And as she laughed, the Speaking Bird told them the whole story, from beginning to end.

The shah hastened back to the city with his newfound children, to release their mother from her unjust captivity and humbly beg her forgiveness. She in turn was so overcome to have her lost children restored to her that she found no room in her heart for bitterness.

As for her cruel sisters, who had lived all these years in pleasure and idleness, their spirits were so curdled with hate and envy when they heard the news that they fell down dead in fits of rage.

The shah and his queen, and their three children, Farid and Faruz and Farizad of the Rose's Smile, lived happily for many years, until at last there came to them, as comes to all, the Destroyer of Delights and Sunderer of Societies, and they became as though they had never been. Glory to the Eternal Lord, who knows no shadow of change!

When Sheherazade had finished this story, she looked long at King Shahryar. He did not say a word, but his eyes were bright with tears.

"The night is long," said King Shahryar. "Will morning never come?"
"Is it not said," asked Sheherazade, "that all things come to one who waits?" And
she related the parable of

TRUE KNOWLEDGE

THERE WAS once a handsome young man who wanted to know everything there was to be known. He spent all his days in the pursuit of learning. At last, there was no one left in his hometown who could teach him anything at all.

A merchant came through town, and the young man eagerly pumped him for any knowledge he might have. The merchant answered all his questions, and finally said, "If you would learn more, you must leave your home. There lives, in a city far from here, the wisest of all men. Like his father and his grandfather before him, he is a blacksmith, and if you want to become his student, you must apprentice yourself to him."

At once the young man put together some food for the journey, took up his stick and his sandals, and set off in search of the wise blacksmith. He journeyed for forty days and forty nights, through all kinds of dangers, and at last he came to the city where the blacksmith lived.

When he came to the forge, he sank to his knees in the dust and kissed the hem of the blacksmith's robe.

"What do you want?" asked the smith.

"Knowledge," answered the young man.

The smith handed the young man the cord of the bellows. "Then pull this," he said.

The young man pulled at the bellows until dusk. The next day the same thing happened, and the next, and the next. For five whole years

he worked the bellows, without another word from his master, or from the other apprentices who were working away at similar tasks.

At last the young man dared to call out, "Master!"

The whole smithy, with its clash and bustle, fell silent. The smith turned to the young man and asked, "What do you want?"

The young man replied, "Knowledge."

The smith turned back to the forge, saying, "Pull the cord."

Another five years passed, in silence and hard work. Occasionally one of the apprentices would write down some question for the blacksmith. Sometimes the smith would throw the note into the flames; sometimes he would put it into his turban. If he threw it into the fire, the question was not worthy of an answer. If he put it into his turban, the apprentice would find the answer that evening, written in letters of gold upon the wall of his bedroom.

At the end of the ten years, the smith came over to the young man and tapped him on the shoulder. "My son," he said, "let go of the cord."

The young man looked up.

"Your apprenticeship is done. You have learned what I have to teach. Return now to your own town. You know as much as I, or as any man. For you have learned the best knowledge of all — patience."

The old smith kissed him good-bye, and the young man went home, neither hurrying nor delaying, but walking at the world's pace.

And on another night, Sheherazade told King Shahryar the story of

PRINCESS NUR AL-NIHAR, THE THREE PRINCES, AND PERI-BANU

LONG AGO, there was a king in India who had three sons: Husain, Ali, and Ahmad. They grew up in their father's palace with their orphan cousin, Princess Nur al-Nihar.

It was the king's intention to marry Nur al-Nihar to some prince, but as his own sons grew up, he realized that all three of them were head-over-heels in love with their beautiful cousin. This worried him, for how could he choose among his own sons? Two of them would be left wounded and sad. But if he found some other suitable husband for her, all three of his sons would be plunged into gloom and despair.

Therefore the king called his sons before him and told them, "My sons, you are all equal in my eyes. I have seen that all three of you love your cousin, the princess Nur al-Nihar. I cannot blame you, for is she not the liveliest and wittiest and loveliest of her sex? But all three of you cannot marry her.

"I have thought of a way in which one of you can win her without losing the love of his brothers. It is this: you must leave my court and go your separate ways. Travel to far countries, and bring back, after one year, the most wondrous thing you find in your wanderings. He who brings back the greatest marvel shall marry Nur al-Nihar, and the other two shall accept my judgment on the matter, and wish their brother and his cousin well."

The three princes, who had also been troubled, readily agreed to this plan. So on the next day, the king provided each of them with as many bags of gold as he wanted for his travels, and sent them on their way, dressed as wandering merchants.

They rode a short way together and, that evening, ate a meal together at an inn. They agreed to part the next morning and, after the space of one year, if they were still living, to meet again at the same inn before returning together to their father and Princess Nur al-Nihar.

The eldest, Prince Husain, set off first. After three months, he reached the kingdom of Bishangarh, on the seacoast of India. He hired the largest room in the most expensive inn, and lay down to rest.

The next day he walked into the city and began to explore the market. It was divided into streets, vaulted over but lit by skylights, and the maze of alleyways was full of rare and expensive goods. Each street was devoted to a single trade. One, for instance, was full of fabrics: silks, satins, brocades, tissues, and even bales of the fine Patna gauzes known as "woven air." In another street, Prince Husain found gems and jewels of every kind: diamonds and rubies, emeralds, pearls, and other precious stones, all so dazzling that they lit up the stores with their brilliance. Everywhere were small boys selling little nosegays of roses and jasmine, and the whole market was full of sweet scents.

Prince Husain came to the street in which prayer carpets were sold. He was resting his legs in one of the shops when a man passed by the door, crying, "Who will buy this carpet? Who will buy? A bargain at thirty thousand gold pieces!"

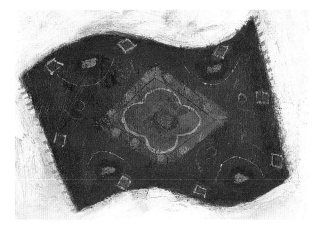

Prince Husain was startled to his feet. "A bargain?" he shouted. "But that's a small fortune!"

The man with the carpet, thinking Prince Husain to be a merchant newly arrived in the city, replied, "Indeed, good sir, but even so, thirty thousand gold pieces is less than this carpet is worth. In fact, my master has instructed me not to part with it for less than forty thousand."

"It must be a special carpet, then," said Husain.

"It is," replied the carpet seller. "It has this virtue: Whoever sits on the carpet and wills himself elsewhere will be transported there in the twinkling of an eye, whether the place be near or far."

Hearing these words, Prince Husain knew that he had found the most wonderful thing he could hope to find. "If what you say is true," he said, "I will pay you forty thousand gold pieces, and an extra thousand for yourself. But my money is at the inn."

"In that case," said the man, "sit with me on the carpet, and wish us there."

No sooner had Prince Husain phrased the words in his mind than the magic carpet lifted itself into the air and transported them back to the inn. So Prince Husain paid over the forty thousand gold pieces, and the extra thousand for the seller to keep, and sat back to congratulate himself on his good fortune. Neither of his brothers could possibly find anything more extraordinary and useful than the magic carpet. Princess Nur al-Nihar was virtually his already.

Husain was strongly tempted to go straight home and claim the princess, but he had agreed to meet his brothers at the end of the year, so he stayed in Bishangarh, attending the court and learning much that was useful from the king of that land. He also visited the many

temples of the city and, just before he left for home, attended the annual festival, to which everyone in the kingdom came.

The king and his court sat in a tower especially constructed for the occasion, painted with images of birds and beasts, and the common people thronged on the plain below them. The high point of the entertainment was a mock battle with a thousand mounted elephants, but instead of soldiers on their backs, there were jugglers and minstrels.

After that magnificent spectacle, Prince Husain lingered no more in Bishangarh, but, sitting himself on his magic carpet, wished himself back to the inn near home, where he set himself to wait for his brothers.

The second brother, Prince Ali, meanwhile had joined a merchants' caravan and journeyed to Persia, where he settled down in the city of Shiraz to search for some marvel to take home to his father. He took lodging in the chief inn, and set out to explore the market.

Here, too, the market was the spicy, bustling heart of the city, with bales of cloth, carpets, jewels, pots, and goods of all kinds being sold in a hubbub of noisy, bartering voices. Only one man remained silent, and he was carrying an ivory tube. Finally, when there was a lull in the general noise, this man suddenly shouted, "A bargain! A bargain!" That soon got the crowd's attention, for there was no one in that market who was not looking for a bargain. The man continued, "Who will buy this ivory tube, for only thirty thousand gold coins?"

At that, the crowd who had stopped to listen laughed and turned away, saying, "The man is a fool."

Prince Ali, however, approached the man, saying, "This tube must have some hidden virtue, to be worth thirty thousand gold coins."

"Indeed it has," answered the man. "So much so, that, although I have opened the bargaining at thirty thousand gold coins, I am forbidden to sell it for less than forty thousand. For the maker of this tube is dead, and there will never be another like it."

"What is its virtue?" asked Prince Ali.

"If you look through this tube," answered the man, "you will see whatever you wish to see, wherever it is."

"If that is true," said the prince, "then the tube is worth what you say, and I will pay you a thousand gold coins in addition for yourself."

The man handed the prince the tube, and Ali looked through it, wishing to see his true love, Princess Nur al-Nihar. He saw her, clear as day! And when he did so, he nearly dropped the precious tube.

The princess was taking her bath. She was sitting among her servants in the hammam, laughing and playing in the water, and looking at herself in a mirror.

The prince said, "If I searched the world over for another ten years, I would never find anything so precious as this." So he paid the man the forty thousand gold coins, and an extra thousand for himself, satisfied that neither of his brothers could ever find anything so wonderful as the spying tube.

Prince Ali, like Prince Husain, had some time to kill before the brothers were due to meet again, and he whiled away some weeks in Persia, learning by heart the most beautiful Persian poems. But at last it was time for him, too, to return home. He found his brother Husain already at the inn, and, not telling each other what things they had found, they settled down to wait for the youngest brother, Prince Ahmad.

Prince Ahmad had set off in his turn in search of a marvel but, although he journeyed far and wide, he could only find ordinary things. At last, however, he came to the city of Samarkand, where he

went at once to the market, to see what rare and precious thing he could find to bring back to his father.

There he heard a man asking thirty thousand gold coins for a single apple. It was true that it was a very large apple, red on one side, and gold on the other, but even so, the man was not finding any takers. People were laughing at him, and jostling him aside in the stream of eager buyers and sellers.

Prince Ahmad approached him, asking, "What is it about this apple that makes it worth such a vast sum?"

The man answered, "The apple is of such value that it really cannot be priced; but I have been instructed to open the bidding at thirty thousand gold coins, and not to accept less than forty thousand."

"Well," said the prince, "it is certainly a handsome apple."

"The looks are nothing to the smell," said the man, "and the smell is nothing to the virtue."

"Let me smell it, then," said Prince Ahmad, "and then you can tell me of its virtue."

The man held the apple beneath the prince's nose, and he breathed in its subtle perfume. The prince nearly swooned. He declared, "Allah be praised! All my weariness has gone. It is as if I had been born again."

"The apple can do more than refresh the weary," said the seller. "It is not a natural fruit, but was made by the hand of man. Its creator was a sage and healer, who spent all his life in the study of plants, herbs, and cures. There is no disease in the world that cannot be cured by smelling this fruit. It can bring someone back from the very brink of death."

At that moment, an old man, blind and paralyzed, was carried past them in the street. Seizing the apple, Prince Ahmad held it beneath the old man's nose. Immediately, the sick man rose up, lithe as a cat, and ran away down the street.

"I will buy the apple for your asking price," said the prince, "and pay you an extra thousand gold coins for yourself."

It had taken Prince Ahmad nearly a full year to find the apple, so he made his way straight home, to meet up with his brothers at the inn.

That night, the three of them dined together, and agreed to show one another what they had found. First, Prince Husain showed the magic carpet, and took his brothers, in the twinkling of an eye, to the far end of the world, and back again.

"This carpet is truly a marvel," said Prince Ali. "But brother, if you look into my spying tube, you will be amazed."

So Prince Husain looked into the ivory tube. Instead of exclaiming with delight, he groaned and turned pale. "There is no hope for any of us," he said, "for Princess Nur al-Nihar is on her deathbed. I have seen her."

"Do not worry," said Prince Ahmad, producing his apple. "This apple will cure all ills."

The three princes immediately climbed aboard the magic carpet, which took them to the room where the princess lay on her bed of torment. The serving women all screamed, but the princes took no notice. Prince Ahmad held the apple beneath her nose, and as the princess breathed in its healing scent, she opened her eyes and smiled. "I feel quite better," she said.

When the king heard the news, he was full of joy, for he had despaired of Princess Nur al-Nihar's life. But he could not decide which of the wonderful things that his sons had brought him was the greatest marvel. "Without the spying glass, you would not have known that the princess was ill," he said. "Without the magic carpet, you could not have reached her. And without the apple, you could not have saved her. Each was essential, yet each would have been useless without the others.

"Therefore I must set you another test, and one that all can judge. Let us have an archery competition. He whose arrow is found to have gone the farthest will win the hand of the princess."

All three of the brothers agreed.

Prince Husain shot first, and his arrow sped into the distance. Prince Ali shot second, and his arrow soared above and beyond his brother's.

Finally Prince Ahmad drew back the bow and, summoning all his strength and skill, let fly. The arrow seemed to have wings, it flew so high, disappearing completely from view.

Although the watchers searched and searched, they could find no sign of where Prince Ahmad's arrow came to earth, and as the king had said that the arrow must be found, he had to declare Prince Ali the winner. Everyone thought that Prince Ahmad's arrow must have gone farther, but it could not be proved.

So Prince Ali and Princess Nur al-Nihar were married, with great celebrations, but neither Prince Husain nor Prince Ahmad attended the feast.

Husain was quite broken at his loss. He renounced the world completely and, apprenticing himself to a wandering holy man, devoted the rest of his life to solitary contemplation.

As for Ahmad, he felt sure he had been cheated of his prize. So he set off in the direction in which he had fired, searching for his arrow. He walked for many miles, finding no trace, and at last he came to a solid barrier of rock, which no arrow could have passed. He cast about, and, sure enough, there was the arrow lying on the ground!

Prince Ahmad knew then that there was some deep mystery at work, for he knew that, unaided, even he could never have fired an arrow so far. He studied the rock face, and saw that there seemed to be the outline of a door in the stone. He pushed idly at this, and, to his amazement, a door swung open.

Prince Ahmad entered the door, and found himself in a magnificent palace. A lady was there, more ravishing even than Princess Nur al-Nihar. "Welcome, Prince Ahmad," she said, and her voice was soft and warm as the breath of the wind on a still summer's night.

"Do not be startled," she continued. "We two have been fated to love since you were born. My name is Peri-Banu, and my father was a jinni, but my mother was a mortal princess. It was I who sold the magic carpet, the ivory tube, and the wonderful apple — the three greatest treasures I possessed — and I who gave wings to your arrow.

"Do not regret your cousin Nur al-Nihar. She will be happiest with your brother Ali; while you, my dear, will be happiest with me. But I warn you: I am my own mistress. I will take orders from no man.

"Do you wish to marry me, and love me?"

"I cannot help but love you," answered Prince Ahmad, his voice trembling with emotion. "And if I could not marry you, and serve you, I should die."

So Prince Ahmad and Peri-Banu were married without more ado, and they lived in great luxury and content in her palace of marvels.

After six months, however, Prince Ahmad, though not wearying of his bride, began to worry about his father the king, whom he had left so abruptly. "I must visit him," he said, and although Peri-Banu was reluctant to let him go, at last she agreed.

But she told him, "Do not on any account tell the king about our marriage, or the wonders of my palace, for only trouble could come of it."

Therefore when Prince Ahmad returned to his father's palace he did not mention Peri-Banu, or say where he had been. He brushed aside his father's questions with a smile, saying, "All that matters is that I am no longer angry about the matter of the archery competition. All is forgiven and forgotten. Hunting my arrow, I found my destiny. Life has opened fair and sweet before me."

But the king was not satisfied with this answer, and could not help brooding over Prince Ahmad's secret. He confided in his wazir, and the wazir replied, "You are right to worry. Remember, both Prince Husain and Prince Ahmad were wounded to the quick by the archery contest at which Prince Ali won the hand of Princess Nur al-Nihar. Prince Husain, we know, has renounced the toil and cares of the world to become a holy man, but as for Prince Ahmad we cannot be sure that he means you no harm. He will not say where he has been, yet he has obviously found a position of wealth and power somewhere. It could be that he is plotting to overthrow you."

Prince Ahmad took leave of his father and set off for home, promising to return the following month. When he left, he was secretly followed by an old sorceress, sent by the king to spy on his son.

The sorceress saw the prince reach the rock face and enter by the hidden door. So one month later, she hid herself outside the door, waiting for Prince Ahmad to come out.

As he rode out, Prince Ahmad saw what he thought was a heap of rags lying in his path. But when he stopped to examine it, he saw it was an old woman, moaning and groaning as if she was near to death. "What is the matter?" he asked.

"Oh, good sir, have pity on an old woman," replied the sorceress. "As I was walking along, I was overtaken by a fever. All my limbs were trembling, and I fell down and cannot get up again."

So Prince Ahmad carried her into the palace, and left her in the care of Peri-Banu while he set off once more to visit his father.

Now Peri-Banu was not so easily fooled as Prince Ahmad, and she soon suspected that the old woman was not so ill as she seemed. Nevertheless she looked after her tenderly, and gave her water from the Lions' Spring to drink, which cures all bodily ills. Then she showed the sorceress the treasures of her palace, before sending her on her way.

The sorceress made good speed back to the king's palace, to tell the king and his wazir what she had found out.

"Surely this is good news," said the king. "If Prince Ahmad is married to one of the jinn, and lives in such a wonderful palace, he will not covet my throne."

"Do not be so sure," said the scheming wazir. "The jinn cannot be trusted, nor can humans who league with them."

"Perhaps you are right," said the king. "I suppose the safest thing would be to throw him into jail while he is here; then he can do me no harm."

"Surely it would be better," said the sorceress, "to ask your son to supply you with some of the wonders that I saw in his palace. That way he would both prove his goodwill, and supply your treasury."

So the king went to Prince Ahmad and said, "Son, now that you are so rich and happy, I am surprised that you have not brought me any presents."

"I had not thought of it, Father," replied the prince. "What would you like?"

"What I really need," said the king, "is a tent I can use when out hunting, which is big enough to house all my retinue, yet folds up small enough to hold in the palm of my hand."

When Prince Ahmad arrived home, he told Peri-Banu of his father's strange request. "I do not know where we will find such a thing," he said.

"Do not trouble yourself," replied Peri-Banu. "I have such a tent in my treasury, and I showed it to the old woman whom you brought here. I thought she was only feigning illness, and now I am sure of it, for apart from you she is the only mortal who has ever set foot in my palace."

Peri-Banu called for her treasurer to bring her the tent. The treasurer was a jinni, of fearsome aspect. It was only three feet tall, and its head was bigger than its body. It had deep set pig's eyes and a hairy snout, and over its shoulder it carried a great iron club.

"Welcome, Shabbar," said Peri-Banu. "I would like you to accompany my husband, Prince Ahmad, to his father's city, and present the king with the wondrous tent. Be sure to pay the king my best respects."

So Prince Ahmad and Shabbar set out once more for the king's palace. When they arrived, the prince went to greet his father. No sooner had he greeted the king, than the jinni bellowed, "Here is the tent!" The pavilion unfurled from its hand, until it covered the whole of the king's gardens.

Although the king was unnerved by Prince Ahmad's monstrous companion, he was nevertheless delighted with his present, and he entered the tent with his wazir, and the sorceress, and the rest of his court.

No sooner were they all inside than Shabbar leaped in among them, crying, "And here are my mistress's respects!" Quick as an eel, the dwarfish jinni skipped among the company wielding his iron club, until the wazir, the sorceress, and the entire court were laid out cold. Only the king was still standing, and he was shaking like a leaf.

"You foolish man," said Shabbar to the king. "You have meddled where you had no business, and you must pay the price. Because you would not trust your son, you have shown that you yourself are not worthy of trust. Therefore you must leave this city today. My master Prince Ahmad will rule as king in your stead, with his fair queen, the lovely Peri-Banu."

So the king left the city with nothing more than he could carry, and was never heard of again. King Ahmad and Queen Peri-Banu ruled long and wisely in his place. As Prince Ali and Princess Nur al-Nihar had taken no part in the plots of the king and the wazir, King Ahmad gave them a rich province of their own to govern. He also sent to his brother Prince Husain, telling him what had happened and offering him a province of his own, but Prince Husain had renounced this world and all its cares and strife, and sent back no reply save the blessing of Allah upon his brothers and their wives.

"Such is the fate of kings who forsake their trust," said King Shahryar.

*And on another night, Sheherazade entertained King Shahryar with the astonishing
tale of*

ALI BABA AND THE FORTY THIEVES

ONCE THERE lived in a certain city in Persia two brothers named Kasim and Ali Baba. They grew up poor, and had to make their own way in the world. Kasim took the easy route, and married a rich girl; Ali Baba took the hard, and married a poor one. So while Kasim lived a life of luxury, and was the owner of a shop packed from floor to ceiling with costly wares, Ali Baba scraped a living as a woodcutter in the forest.

Every day, Ali Baba went out with his three donkeys to cut wood. Now one day, he was out about his business when he saw a dust cloud billowing up into the air and heard the sound of galloping hooves. Fearing bandits, he hid his donkeys in the bushes and climbed up a tree to get a better look.

Soon the horsemen came into view. There were forty of them, riding hard, and each one looked wickeder than the last. They were indeed a band of robbers, fresh from plundering some caravan. They dismounted and filed past Ali Baba's tree to a large rock nearby, while Ali Baba held his breath and hoped no one would look up.

When the thieves reached the rock, their leader shouted, "Open Sesame!" At these magic words, the rock gaped open, and the thieves walked through, carrying their saddlebags bulging with booty.

After some time, the thieves came out again, with their empty saddlebags, and when all forty had come through, the leader shouted, "Shut Sesame!" and the door closed up.

Ali Baba stayed in his tree until he was quite sure that the thieves had ridden off. He knew he really ought to fetch his donkeys and go home, praising Allah for a lucky escape, but his curiosity, and his destiny, led him to the rock. There was no sign of any door or entrance in it, and Ali Baba could not work out how to enter. But he couldn't just leave it at that, so he decided to try saying the words he had heard. He didn't shout them — in fact his voice was a mere trembling whisper — but still at "Open Sesame!" the doorway opened up, and Ali Baba stumbled through it.

Inside, he found a large cave, filled with light and air filtering down from holes in the rock above. It was the perfect robbers' hideout, and it was crammed with the spoils of years of thievery: bales of silk, piles of richly woven carpets, heaps of jewels, and sacks of gold coins.

Ali Baba wasted no time, but hauled out as many of the sacks of coins as his donkeys could carry. Once outside, he cried, "Shut Sesame!" and the doorway closed. He loaded the gold onto his donkeys, covering it up with brushwood to hide it from prying eyes.

When he arrived home, Ali Baba called excitedly to his wife, "Look what Allah has sent us!" Taking the bags one by one, he poured their contents in an unending golden stream onto the floor.

"Quick," said Ali Baba, "help me dig a hole and bury this treasure so that no one will see it."

"Gladly," said his wife. "But first I must weigh it, to see how much there is."

So Ali Baba's wife went around to the house of his brother Kasim, the merchant, to ask Kasim's wife to lend her a pair of scales. Now Kasim's wife always had to know everything that was going on and, sensing some mystery here, smeared the underside of the scales with suet so that some part of whatever was weighed was bound to stick there.

Ali Baba's wife took the scales home, and carefully weighed the gold pieces in the scales, making a black mark on the wall for each full load. Then she and Ali Baba emptied all the gold into the ditch he had dug, and buried it safely.

However, neither of them noticed the single gold coin that had stuck to the scales, which they returned to Kasim's wife.

As soon as they had gone, that scheming shrew upturned the scales, expecting to see some beans, or grains of barley. When she saw the gold coin, she nearly had a fit. She yelled for her husband, who came at a run, as he had learned was wise at times like this. "Look at this, you oaf, you fool, you blubber brain! There you are rubbing your fat stomach and preening your greasy hair, telling yourself what a fine figure of a gentleman you are, and that little rat, your brother, who's supposed to be so poor he eats little better than his donkeys, has so much gold he needs to borrow my scales to weigh it! He obviously has more than he can count! Go away, and don't come back until you've forced that lying scoundrel to tell where he got the money. Perhaps your father was secretly rich, and Ali Baba has been hoarding your inheritance all this time."

So Kasim, who was himself quite ill with jealousy and spite at the thought of Ali Baba's wealth, took himself off to his brother's house.

Kasim found Ali Baba in the courtyard and, seizing him by the throat, began to shake him violently, shouting, "Where did you get the money? Where did you get the money?"

Poor Ali Baba could hardly get his breath when Kasim finally let him go, but, seeing that his secret had been discovered, and remembering that Kasim was, after all, his brother and boyhood companion, he managed to splutter out the story of the forty thieves and their cave full of treasure.

"Even though you have never reached out your hand to help me," he said, "you are my brother. Therefore, as Allah has been generous to me, so will I be to you. You can have half of my gold, with my blessing."

"That will do for a start," said Kasim. "But you must also tell me where this cave is, and the magic words for opening and closing the door, so that I can see it for myself. Otherwise I will have to carry out my citizen's duty and report you to the police as an associate of thieves."

Ali Baba had no choice but to tell his wicked brother everything.

Leading ten mules, Kasim set out for the cave. He came to the rock, cried, "Open Sesame!" and ventured in, the door closing behind him. When he saw the treasure trove he went quite wild with greed. He threw himself down and rolled around in the gold and jewels, in an ecstasy of money lust.

At last he came back to his senses, and began to stack up bags by the door to load onto his mules. When he judged he had as much as they could carry, he stopped, resolving to come back next time with a whole train of camels. But when he tried to open the door, he found that, in his excitement and fever, he had utterly forgotten the magic words. "It's something to do with grain," he muttered, scratching his head.

So Kasim puffed himself up as grand and imposing as he could, and said solemnly, "Open Barley!" And when that didn't work, he tried, "Open Oats!" and "Open Beans!" and "Open Rye!" and "Open Chickpea!" In fact, he tried the name of every cereal and seed that the hand of the Sower had cast upon the fields since the birth of time, save only sesame, which had vanished from his mind as if he had never heard the word.

So Kasim was left to tremble and shake behind that cruel door until the forty thieves came back to the cave and, finding an intruder there, cut him into six pieces with their swords.

The thieves were in an utter fury that a stranger should have entered their cave. They just couldn't understand it, as they had no idea that Ali Baba had spied on them from the tree. But they felt safe that at least the man who had had the impudence to try to rob them was dead.

They put the gold that he had stacked up back with the main treasure, never noticing that the sacks that Ali Baba had taken were missing. Nevertheless, when they went out again to plunder and rob, they left Kasim's mutilated body inside the door as a warning to anyone else who dared to trespass in their hideout.

Now Kasim was certainly a greedy and selfish man, who deserved no better than he got, but his wife was just as bad. She had spent all day imagining all the things she was going to spend their new wealth on. Her daydreams had been interrupted only once, by a poor crippled beggar at her kitchen door, and she soon sent him away with a flea in his ear. "Get away, you filthy vagabond," she shouted, "or I'll call the police. These are hard enough times for honest folk, without having to deal with idle spongers like you!" For whatever she intended to do with the thieves' treasure, it was certain none of it was going to be given away.

When Kasim failed to come home with his mules laden with gold, she began to worry. At last she could bear it no more, and went to Ali Baba's house to see if he knew what had become of Kasim. They waited all night, and in the morning, when Kasim had still not come, she wheedled Ali Baba into going out into the forest to search for him.

Ali Baba went out with his three donkeys, fully expecting to run into his brother on the way, but found no sign of him. So he arrived at the rock and, gathering up his courage, said very quietly, "Open Sesame!"

The doorway opened, and there, inside, was Kasim, neatly cut up into six pieces. Ali Baba was nearly too sick at the sight to remember to gather up some more coins, but not quite. So he loaded his brother's remains onto one of his donkeys, and some more booty onto the other two, and went back by the way he had come.

Ali Baba left the two treasure-laden donkeys at his own house, but carried on with the other to Kasim's house. There he was met by the resourceful servant girl, Morgiana. He showed her the terrible fate that had met Kasim, and said, "We must keep this quiet. Pretend your master is ill, and go to the druggist today and tomorrow, asking for medicines. On the third day, we can announce his death. But if we are to make sure that those thieves never find out about us, we must be certain that there is no talk in the city about the way in which my poor brother was butchered."

Morgiana said, "Leave it to me."

So Ali Baba made his way into the house to tell his brother's widow the bad news. She wept and wailed and flung herself on the floor, all the while making sure that Ali Baba — who after all was now much the richest man in the city — saw how fetchingly her eyes welled with tears. "Who will look after me now?" she cried. "Must I live all alone and unprotected?"

Ali Baba seemed completely taken in by this show of grief. "I will look after you," he said, "for you were my brother's wife. My wife and I will move in with you, so that you will not be alone."

Meanwhile, Morgiana the servant girl had been busy. She had visited the druggist to buy medicines, and then she had gone to the weather-beaten old tailor Baba Mustafa. She went into his shop, handed him a gold coin, and said, "Blindfold your eyes." Then she gave him another gold coin and said, "Follow me." When they arrived back at Kasim's house, she took him to the corpse. She gave him another gold coin and said, "Sew up this body as if it were new." Lastly, she gave him a fourth gold coin, saying, "Sew a shroud for the body, and leave." And all this, Baba Mustafa did, wondering greatly.

On the third day, Kasim's funeral was held. Morgiana had been so clever, no one suspected anything.

When the forty thieves returned to their cave, they were astounded to find that Kasim's corpse was gone, and that some of their gold was missing. The leader said, "Men, our secret is known. If we are not to lose all the treasure that generations of our forefathers, robbers all, have stored in this cave, we must find out who it is who possesses the key to our door, and do away with him. One of you must go to the city, disguised as a holy man, and try to find out if anything is known about the funeral of a man who had been cut into six parts. That should cause some talk!"

For days the thief lurked about the streets of the city without hearing anything. He was almost ready to give up, when he passed Baba Mustafa's shop. Noticing the old man sewing in the dark, he complimented him on his nimble fingers. "I may be old," replied the tailor, "but I can still sew up the six pieces of a corpse into a man's shape, blindfolded."

Then the robber knew that he was on the track. "Where was this?" he asked.

"I could not say," said Baba Mustafa, "but I could take you there, if I was blindfolded again, and a gold coin was put in my hand."

Baba Mustafa led the thief through the winding warren of lanes all the way to Kasim's — now Ali Baba's — house. The robber put a chalk mark on the door so that he would know the house again, and went off to tell his fellow thieves that he had found the house of their enemy. But when he tried to lead them there, they were foiled once again by Morgiana's cunning. For she, suspecting some trickery at work when she saw the chalk mark, had taken care to put a similar mark on every house in the street, so that the thieves were utterly bamboozled.

The robber chief sent another of the thieves to ask Baba Mustafa to guide him to Ali Baba's house. This time he marked the door in red; but Morgiana played the same trick.

So on the third occasion, the robber chief himself undertook the task. He stared long and hard at Ali Baba's house, till he was sure he would know it again. Then he returned to the cave, and said, "I have a plan. Let us take forty large earthenware jars, and fill one to the brim with olive oil. You men will each hide in one of the other jars, with your knives and swords at the ready. I will disguise myself as an oil merchant, and we will visit this house. In the night, when all are asleep, you shall rise from the jars, and visit our vengeance on this upstart thief."

The thirty-nine thieves hid themselves in the oil jars, and their leader led them on a string of horses into the city. He stopped at Ali Baba's house and, introducing himself as a stranger to the city, begged to be allowed to store his jars that night in Ali Baba's courtyard. Ali Baba, who was a generous man, said, "Of course, of course. And you must be our guest tonight."

That evening, Morgiana happened to run out of oil. Thinking that there was plenty of oil in the jars in the courtyard, she decided to help herself to a little. But when she approached the first jar, she heard from inside it a voice asking, "Is it time?"

Morgiana, quick as a flash, understood what was going on. "Not yet," she whispered.

The same thing happened at every jar until the last, which was full of oil. So Morgiana built a fire in the courtyard and boiled the oil, and then, with her ladle, poured the boiling oil through the breath holes into the thirty-nine jars, and killed every one of the thieves.

At midnight the robber chief woke and, leaning from his window, clapped his hands to signal his men. When they did not respond, he went down into the courtyard, very angry, to wake them, only to discover them scalded and stifled in the jars. So he climbed over the wall and ran away, seeing that the game was up.

The next morning, Morgiana calmly showed Ali Baba the results of her night's work, and he showered her with thanks. "Now we are safe, thanks to you," he said.

But Morgiana replied, "Do not speak too soon: for remember, the leader of these men has escaped, and may still work some mischief."

But Ali Baba was a happy-go-lucky sort of man, and he couldn't let something like that worry him for long — not when he had the cleverest servant girl in the world, and a fortune kings would envy.

What he most liked was entertaining and sharing his wealth with others. So when his eldest son came home one day, talking about the new friend he had made in the market, Hasan, Ali Baba said carelessly, "Ask the fellow to dinner. I'd like to meet him."

That night, Ali Baba's son brought the merchant, Hasan, back to the house. Hasan greeted Ali Baba warmly, but said, "Alas! I cannot accept your hospitality, for my doctor has told me never to eat food prepared with salt."

"That is no problem," replied Ali Baba. "Morgiana, the servant girl, can certainly prepare a feast without salt; nothing is too difficult for her." So Hasan agreed to stay to dinner.

Now Morgiana was intrigued by this strange guest, who would not eat salt, for she understood that if a man did not take salt with his host he was under no obligation to Allah to behave as a guest should. So she took care to watch him closely, and she saw, as Ali Baba and his son did not, the curved knife that he kept hidden beneath his robe and fingered longingly when he thought no one was looking.

After dinner, Ali Baba, his son, and their guest were relaxing and chatting away when, much to Ali Baba's surprise, Morgiana entered

the room in the filmy costume of a dancing girl, right down to the jade-hilted dagger that dancers wear.

She danced before them with the grace and quickness of a bird, flitting here, there, down to the ground, up again. She danced the dance of the veils, as it is danced before kings and sultans. And at the climax of the dance, she flung herself toward the watchers, and stabbed her dagger into Hasan's heart.

"What have you done?" cried Ali Baba, appalled.

But Morgiana answered, unashamed, "This man was no merchant, but the robber chief. Look under his robe, and you will find the knife with which he would have cut your throat before this night was done."

When Ali Baba understood that Hasan, the oil merchant, and the captain of the forty thieves were all one and the same man, and that Morgiana had saved him once again, he exclaimed, "Morgiana, you are the jewel of all women!" And to show his gratitude, he married her to his son.

A year passed before Ali Baba felt it safe to go once more to the robbers' cave. This time he took Morgiana and his son with him. Once more he called, "Open Sesame!" Once more the doorway in the rock obeyed the call. They carried from the cave every scrap of cloth, every jewel, every coin, every treasure, and took it all home with them, the loot of centuries.

And so Ali Baba, through the chance of fate, the bounty of Allah, and the quick wits of a servant girl, rose from being the poorest woodcutter in the city, to the richest man.

"There are no girls like Morgiana nowadays," said King Shahryar. "I should know, for I have married so many, searching for one."

"Perhaps not," said Sheherazade.

"Your tales are full of wisdom and delight," said King Shahryar. "But the world is full of misery and foolishness."

"It is said," replied Sheherazade, "that the caliph Harun al-Rashid often felt the same, and that he kept about his court a jester, Buhlul, to remind him that though a ruler must care for his people, yet he must not take the cares of the world upon himself."

And she told him the story called

HOW MANY FOOLS?

ONE DAY the caliph was in one of his dark, brooding moods. All his plans had gone awry. He said angrily to Buhlul, "How many fools can there be in Baghdad?"

"Too many to count," laughed Buhlul.

"Count them anyway," snapped Harun. "I want a list."

Buhlul was not overfond of work, but his quick wits soon found a way out of the task. "I tell you what," he said, "I will make you a list of all the wise men in Baghdad. Those who aren't on it are the fools."

Buhlul, like jesters all over the world, prided himself on taking liberties in his master's presence. Once, Harun offered him a thousand dinars. He refused the gift. Harun offered them again, and again Buhlul refused. When Harun asked him why, he just stretched out his legs, sprawling in insolent silence.

The officers of the court would have had him beaten for his rude manner, but Harun questioned him again about why he should behave so strangely.

"Well, you see," said Buhlul, "if I had stretched out my hand to take your money, I wouldn't have been able to stretch out my legs to take my ease."

On another day, Buhlul accompanied Harun al-Rashid on one of his
war forays. Buhlul entered the caliph's tent, and found him parched
and desperate for a cup of water.

Buhlul fetched the drink, and gave it to Harun, who gulped the
liquid down.

"Tell me," said Buhlul, "if we had been in the driest desert, with no
water to be had, how much would you have given me for that cup?"

"Half my kingdom," said Harun.

A little later, Harun stepped outside to relieve himself.

"Tell me," said Buhlul, when the caliph returned, "if by some magic,
I had been able to cause your body to retain that liquid, how much
would you have given me to lift the spell?"

"Half my kingdom," said Harun.

"Do you mean to say," replied Buhlul, "that you plunge us into this
tangle of cares, and these bloody wars, for an empire you would trade
for a swig of water and a moment of relief?"

And the caliph wept.

For a thousand nights, Sheherazade beguiled King Shahryar with her stories, winning each night a stay of execution until the next. Some of the stories made him laugh; some of them made him cry. Some were romantic; some were coarse. Some were full of foolishness; some were full of wisdom. She told him the story of the birds and the beasts and the son of Adam, and the story of the angel of death and the rich king. And on the thousand and first night, she told him about

THE KEYS OF DESTINY

IT IS said that Muhammad Ibn Thailun, sultan of Egypt, was as wise and good a ruler as his father had been cruel and unjust. Therefore Allah blessed his reign, and the land and the people prospered.

One day, at the beginning of his reign, Muhammad called all the officers of his court before him to question them about their duties and see whether they were paid enough, or too much, for what they did.

The first to come before him were the wazirs, forty old men with long white beards and wise eyes, led by the grand wazir. Then the governors of the various provinces, and the captains of the army and of the police. One by one they knelt before their sultan and kissed the ground, while he rewarded some for their faithful work, and rebuked others for slackness or dishonesty.

Then came the headsman, carrying the sword of justice. But instead of walking in proudly, with the naked blade held high, the man crept in with his head hanging down, and the sword languishing in its sheath. Prostrating himself before the sultan, he said, "Surely the day of justice has dawned for me! For, my lord, in the days of your father, this sword was never in its sheath. There were scarcely enough hours in the day to execute judgment on all the criminals, traitors, and ne'er-do-wells who were sent before me. My life was a happy and busy one. But now, time hangs heavy on my hands. If this land remains so peaceful and content, I shall surely die of hunger. But Allah grant our master long life!"

Sultan Muhammad answered, "We come from Allah, and return to him! It is true that good for one may mean ill for another. But lift up your heart, headsman. I shall award you a salary equal to the gifts that you used to receive from those poor unfortunates my father used to send you. I hope that your sword may rust away before it is next required."

At last there was only one wrinkled old man left. The sultan called him over, and asked, "What do you do?"

The old man replied, "O King of time, I have but one duty. I guard a casket that your father entrusted to me. For this I receive ten gold coins from the treasury every month."

"That is high pay for such easy work!" said the sultan. "What is in the casket?"

"I have guarded it for forty years," said the old man, "and I do not know."

"Then bring it to me," said the sultan.

The old man went away and came back shortly with a chest of carved gold. "Open it," ordered the sultan.

Inside the casket was a little bright red earth and a manuscript, inscribed in gold on the purple-stained skin of a gazelle.

The sultan took the manuscript and tried to read it, but, though he knew many of the tongues of man, he could not make it out, nor could any of the wise and learned men of his court. He called on all the famous sages of Egypt, Syria, Persia, and India to read the writing, but none of them could read it. What are sages after all, but foolish old men in large turbans?

But at last a wizened servant tottered forward, saying, "Lord, I served your father for many years, and I can tell you the history of this manuscript. Your father stole it from Sheikh Hasan Abdallah al-Ashar, but then found, as you have found, that nobody could read it. So he tried to force the sheikh to read it for him, and when Sheikh Hasan Abdallah refused, he threw him into the deepest dungeon in the palace. Allah alone knows whether he groans there still, or is now dead, for all this happened forty years ago."

Sultan Muhammad called the captain of the guard, and told him to make a search of all the dungeons to see if the Sheikh was still alive. It was not long before Sheikh Hasan Abdallah was found, chained to a wall in a dank, dark cell.

He was dressed in new robes, given a staff to lean on, and brought before the sultan. When Sultan Muhammad saw the old sheikh, his face lined with the suffering of forty years of unjust captivity, he took the old man's hand, saying, "Forgive me, I beg you, for your cruel punishment. I have only today learned your story. This manuscript, I believe, is yours, and I wish to return it to you."

The old sheikh fell to his knees, crying, "Allah is wise, who makes the poison and the antidote to flower in the same field. Forty years I have lain in the dark; now, the son of my enemy stretches out his hand to me, beckoning me into the sunlight."

Then Sheikh Hasan Abdallah said, "For this manuscript, I risked my life. It was the only thing I brought with me from Many-Columned Iram, the fabled city of Shaddad bin Ad, where no man may set his feet. Your father tried to force me to read it, and I would not. But for you, who freely return it, I will tell you what is written here."

Sheikh Hasan Abdallah paused for breath. "This manuscript," he said, "contains the beginning and end of all wisdom. Its story is the story of my own life.

"My father was one of the richest merchants in Cairo, and I was his only son. He gave me the best of educations, and married me to a beautiful young girl, with eyes like pools of starlight. My wife and I lived together in delight for ten happy years.

"But no man can escape his destiny. After ten years, my father died. The ships on which his fortune depended were all wrecked in a storm at sea, and the warehouses in which his goods were stored were all destroyed by fire. I was reduced to wretched poverty, and could only live by begging for crusts outside the mosques.

"One day when I was on my way to beg, I met a Bedouin mounted on a red camel. When he saw me, he stopped and asked, 'Can you direct me to the house of the rich merchant named Hasan Abdallah al-Ashar?'

"I have never felt so ashamed. I answered, 'I know of no such man.'

"But the Bedouin leaped down from his camel, crying, 'But are you not yourself the man I seek?'

"I had to admit that I was. The man accompanied me home and, seeing our poverty, gave me ten gold pieces to buy food. He remained with me as my guest for sixteen days, and each day he gave me another ten gold pieces.

"At the end of this time, the Bedouin asked me, 'Are you willing to serve me?'

"'I am already your slave,' I replied.

"'In that case, sell yourself to me,' he said. 'I will pay you fifteen hundred gold pieces, which will keep your family fed for many years, if you will sell yourself as my slave.'

"He must have seen that I suspected the worst, for he continued, 'Do not be afraid. I shall not take your life, or your freedom. All I require is your companionship on a long journey that I must make.'

"So I agreed to his strange request.

"On the next morning, I accompanied my master to the beast market and bought myself a camel, and provisions for a long journey.

"Soon we were in the desert. We rode on without ceasing through the trackless wastes where none but Allah dwells. My master guided us, by some secret knowledge, through the sea of sand, and each day under the burning sky was as long as a night of evil dreams.

"On the eleventh morning, we came to a plain, where the golden sands of the desert seemed to have turned silver. In the middle of this plain was a high column, on the top of which was the copper statue of a young man. His right hand was extended, and from each of his fingers dangled a heavy key. The first key was of gold, the second of silver, the third of copper, the fourth of iron, and the fifth of lead.

"I knew nothing of these keys, but my master knew. They were the Keys of Destiny, and whoever possesses them must bear the fate of each.

"The Bedouin said, 'Now is your chance to buy back your liberty. All you must do is take your bow and shoot down the keys.'

"I shot with all my skill, and with my first arrow brought down the golden key, which is the Key of Misery. 'You may keep that for yourself,' said my master, so I tucked it into my belt.

"With my second shot, I brought down the silver key, which is the Key of Suffering. 'You may keep that, too,' said my master.

"My next two arrows brought down the keys of iron and of lead, the Key of Glory and the Key of Happiness and Wisdom. These my master pounced on in delight.

"I aimed my bow at the last key, but my master cried, 'Stop, you foolish man!' For the copper key is the Key of Death. I was so startled at his cry that I shot myself in the foot with my own arrow, and that was the start of my suffering and my misery.

"For three days we rode on through the desert, and all the time my foot was causing me agony. Then we came into a fertile oasis with fruit trees, and I picked one of the fruits. No sooner had I bitten into it than my jaws were stuck together. For three days I could neither eat nor drink and, when my teeth finally came unstuck, I found that my master had eaten all my food and drunk all my water.

"We stopped that night at the foot of a high mountain. The Bedouin told me, 'Now is your chance to repay me for my kindness to you and your family. Climb to the top of this mountain, and wait for the sun to rise. At dawn, turn to the east and recite the morning prayer; then you may come down. But do not fall asleep, for the ground up there is poisonous.'

"Despite my pain, hunger, and thirst, I knew that I did owe my master much, so I dragged myself to the top of the hill. But I was so tired when I got there that I could not help falling deep asleep.

"At dawn, I woke in the most terrible pain. My entire body was

swollen and aching, and I was feverish; I had been poisoned by that noxious place. But I forced myself to rise and make the morning prayer; my shadow loomed out to the west.

"I started to descend the mountain, but could not keep my feet. I fell, and rolled all the way down, adding bruises and cuts to the rest of my ills. I landed at my master's feet and all he said was, 'Ah, there you are! Come and help me dig. At the farthest point where your shadow touched the ground, we shall find a great treasure.'

"We dug, and uncovered a marble tomb, with an inscription that I could not read. Inside the tomb we found human bones and a manuscript, inscribed in gold on the purple-stained skin of a gazelle. You hold it in your hands, O King of time.

"My master, who had much hidden knowledge, could read the manuscript. As he did so, his eyes began to sparkle with an inner fire. 'Now I know the way!' he cried. 'Hasan Abdallah, rejoice! We shall be the first of mortal men to set foot in Many-Columned Iram, the city of Shaddad bin Ad. There we shall find the red powder that makes it possible to turn base metals into precious ones. We shall be rich!'

"'I do not want to be rich,' I replied. 'I just want to feel better.'

"'Nonsense,' said the Bedouin. But he did stop long enough to harvest some cacti, whose broad, spiky leaves concealed juicy flesh that satisfied both hunger and thirst.

"As soon as we had refreshed ourselves, we remounted our camels. We rode for three days and three nights, following the directions in the manuscript, until we came to a glittering river, which threw back the rays of the sun like a mirror. It was a river of mercury, and it was spanned only by a slender crystal bridge with no handrail. It was so narrow and steep that only an idiot would have set foot on it.

"My master stepped confidently onto the bridge, and I had to follow, trusting in the mercy of Allah.

"We came safely to the other side, and walked on for some hours, until we came to the entrance to a black valley, in the murk of which I could see the dark shapes of serpents, and worse.

"I cast myself to the ground in despair. But the Bedouin cried, 'Be brave! You are not going to

die, but will return to Cairo richer than the sultan himself. You must perform just one more task.'

"'What is that?' I asked.

"'You must enter the valley and wait until you see a vast serpent with black horns. Using your skill with the bow, you must slay it, and bring me its brain and heart. Leave the rest to me.'

"When I came back with the head and heart of that dread creature, still trembling with terror and exhaustion, the Bedouin took them from me without a word. He had built a fire with dry grass and dead wood, and now he took a diamond from his pocket and, concentrating the rays of the sun through it, kindled flame.

"Then he produced an iron pot and a small ruby phial. 'In this phial,' he said, 'is the blood of the phoenix.' He uncorked the phial and poured its contents into the iron pot, together with the heart and brain of the serpent. Then he put the pot on the fire and, opening the manuscript, began to mutter unintelligible words.

"Suddenly he rose to his feet and bared his shoulders. He ordered me to rub his shoulders with the mixture in the pot, and, as I did so, wings began to sprout from his shoulder blades. They grew and grew until, when he flapped them, he began to rise from the ground. Fearing to be left behind, I clutched at his legs, so when he soared into the sky, I was carried up, too.

"I do not know how long we flew, but at length we found ourselves above a mighty plain of powdered gold, in the midst of which rose a wonderful city of palaces and gardens.

"'At last!' cried the Bedouin. 'Many-Columned Iram, city of dreams, into which no man has ever set foot. Come!' And with that, he swooped down into the city. As soon as we landed, his wings disappeared.

"No words of mine can describe that place. It was built of every precious stone, and at its heart was a garden where the air was scented with musk and the flowers were fed by rivers of wine, of rose essence, and of honey. In a pavilion in that garden was a throne of gold and ruby, and on that throne was the small gold casket that you now hold, O Sultan.

"The Bedouin took the casket and opened it. It was full of red powder. He cried out in exultation, 'See! Here is the vital ingredient that I have sought for so many years!'

"I said, 'Master, throw away the dirty stuff, and fill the box with some of the jewels that lie in heaps all over this city.'

"He answered, 'Fool, this powder is the very soul of riches. A single grain of it can turn any metal into pure gold. With this box, I can rule the world, and turn kings into slaves!'

"I asked him, 'And can this powder add a single day to your life, or buy back a single day of your past?'

"He replied, 'Allah alone is great.'

"We left that city, carrying nothing but the casket of powder and the manuscript. The Bedouin forbade me to take any of the jewels that tempted me at every turn, telling me that to filch a single one would bring instant death.

"And so we returned to Cairo. Ill health and ill luck dogged every step of my way, while my master whistled along without a care. And when I found my home again, it was to learn that my beloved wife and children, for whom I had sold myself into slavery, were all dead. For I still carried at my belt, though I did not know it, the Keys of Misery and Suffering.

"So I went to live with the Bedouin in his palace on the banks of the Nile — no longer his slave, but instead his companion. He taught me much of the hidden science, including the skill to read the magical tongue in which the manuscript is written, though he would not let me read the manuscript itself. He taught me, too, all he knew of the science of alchemy, and let me help him use the precious red powder to turn base metal into gold.

"For all the Bedouin's kindness, I did not prosper, but remained racked by misfortunes of all kinds, while he seemed to live a charmed life, like one who, on earth, is already in paradise.

"But death comes to all, and, one day, I found him lying senseless, with the smile on his face of one born under a happy star. I mourned his loss, and when I buried him I shed tears as for a father.

"I was his heir, so it fell to me to sort out his affairs. I opened the gold casket, the source of his wealth, and found that most of its contents had been used up. All that remains is the powder that you see there now.

"I was not concerned with that, but I was eager to read the

153

precious manuscript, which I had never been allowed to see. When I had read it, I understood why. For the manuscript, which tells the wise how to enter Many-Columned Iram, also tells of the Keys of Destiny, and so at last I understood that the Bedouin had needed me not for my skill with a bow, but to keep the Keys of Misery and Suffering, leaving him the Glory, the Happiness, and the Wisdom.

"At once, I snatched the fateful keys from my belt and melted them down in a crucible. Then I searched everywhere for the other two keys, but I could not find them.

"Before I could enjoy any of my new wealth, I was arrested by your father, Sultan Thailun, who had heard that I had the secret of turning base metal into gold. He took the casket of red powder, and the manuscript, and tried to force me to tell him their uses. When I would not, he cast me into prison."

"What an extraordinary tale!" exclaimed Sultan Muhammad. "It seems to me that, even without the Bedouin's keys, you have found your share of wisdom, and now deserve your share of glory and happiness. Therefore you shall be my grand wazir. Together, we shall use the rest of the red powder to make gold, and with that gold we shall build a mosque in praise of Allah, the all-knowing, the compassionate, who lives and does not die!"

Then Sheherazade lapsed into silence. King Shahryar, much moved by her tale, said, "Truly, each man carries his fate around his neck, and cannot escape it."

Sheherazade said nothing.

King Shahryar said, "Come, tell me a lighter tale."

And Sheherazade said, "I have told all of my tales. Now you can cut off my head."

But King Shahryar replied, "We come from Allah, and return to him. Let the headsman's sword rust in its sheath. For, just as the red powder turned base metal into gold, your stories, Sheherazade, have turned my base desires into love, which is all the wealth any man needs."

A Note on THE ARABIAN NIGHTS

The stories told by Sheherazade to King Shahryar over a thousand and one nights have a long and tangled history. Oral in origin, the stories date back to a lost collection of Persian tales *circa* A.D. 850, but the collection as we know it today mixes stories of Indian, Persian, Arabic, and even European sources.

The first Western translation was made by Antoine Galland, a Frenchman, and published between 1704 and 1715. An English version appeared almost immediately, and stories such as "Aladdin" and "Ali Baba and the Forty Thieves" soon became widely popular.

There is no single authoritative version, and even editions as complete as Sir Richard F. Burton's sixteen-volume *Plain and Literal Translation of the Arabian Nights' Entertainments, Now Entituled the Book of the Thousand Nights and a Night* (Benares: Printed for the Kamashastra Society, 1885-8) cannot be regarded as definitive. But it is Burton's translation on which I have most depended, and no one could compare my text and his without at once seeing the immense debt I owe him.

Burton's translation is — despite its contorted archaic style — the classic English rendering of *The Arabian Nights;* it in turn owes much to the version by Burton's friend John Payne which appeared 1882-4. Burton and Payne braved the disapproval of Victorian society by including in their versions the erotic and coarse episodes which earlier translators (such as E. W. Lane, whose translation was published 1839-41) had omitted. By doing so they risked prosecution, which is why Burton's privately subscribed edition claims to be printed in Benares, India — actually, Stoke Newington, London — for the Kamashastra Society, which did not exist.

Burton's edition was followed by another "complete," but very different version, translated by E. Powys Mathers from the French of Dr. J. C. Mardrus (*The Thousand Nights and One Night,* London: George Routledge & Sons, 1937), on which I have also drawn. More recently, Arabic scholars have provided us with more authentic, less highly spiced, versions, in N. J. Dawood's *Tales from the Thousand and One Nights* (London, New York, and Toronto: Penguin, 1973) and Husain Haddawy's *The Arabian Nights* (New York: W. W. Norton & Co., 1990; London: Everyman's Library, 1992). Professor Haddawy's excellent version translates from the earliest, least suspect text, edited by Muhsin Mahdi as *Alf Layla wa Layla* (Leiden, 1984). It is a work both of scholarship and literature, though many readers may be dismayed to find it lacks almost any of the stories — such as "Aladdin," "Ali Baba and the Forty Thieves," and "Sinbad the Sailor" — which they most associate with *The Arabian Nights*.

My own retelling of a selection of the best stories cannot, of course, claim to be either complete or authentic. I have left out Sinbad, on the grounds both of length and tedium, but retained most of the other best-known tales; I have allowed myself a fairly free rein in reshaping the stories for a modern audience, and in the spelling of proper names; but I have tried to retain the spirit of the tales. There have been many previous attempts to retell the stories for children, from the eighteenth century onward, and those interested in such things might like to compare mine with those of Andrew Lang (*The Arabian Nights Entertainments*, London: Longmans, Green, & Co., 1898, reprinted New York: Dover Books, 1969), Kate Douglas Wiggin and Nora A. Smith (*The Arabian Nights: Their Best-Known Tales*, New York: Charles Scribner's, and London: T.W. Laurie, 1909), and Geraldine McCaughrean (*One Thousand and One Arabian Nights*, Oxford, Toronto, and Melbourne: Oxford University Press, 1982).

No other work exudes such pure joy in storytelling itself as *The Arabian Nights*. Sheherazade herself saves her life by telling stories, and many characters in the tales follow her example. The stories are the most magical thing in this compendium of tales crammed with magic.

Some of the tales, such as "Aladdin," are familiar from countless retellings, and stage and screen versions. Others may seem familiar because they are related to other stories we know. "The Anklet," for instance, is a variant of "Cinderella"; "The Ebony Horse" is essentially Chaucer's "Squire's Tale"; "The Speaking Bird, the Singing Tree, and the Golden Water" is widespread as a folktale known to folklorists as "The Three Golden Sons."

For those who wish to know more about *The Arabian Nights*, Burton's monumental edition, with its abundance of quirky commentary, is not a bad place to start, but it should be supplemented with Haddawy's translation, and with two works of scholarship: Peter L. Caracciolo (ed.), *The Arabian Nights in English Literature* (London: Macmillan, and New York: St. Martin's Press, 1988), and Robert Irwin, *The Arabian Nights: A Companion* (London: Allen Lane, The Penguin Press, 1994).

NEIL PHILIP